The Bushwhacked Piano

Thomas McGuane is the author of several highly acclaimed novels, including *The Sporting Club*; *Ninety-Two in the Shade*, which was nominated for the National Book Award; *Panama*; *Nobody's Angel*; *Something to Be Desired*; *To Skin a Cat*, a collection of short stories; and *An Outside Chance*, a collection of essays on sport. *The Bushwhacked Piano* has won the Hilda Rosenthal Award of the American Academy and Institute of Arts and Letters. His books have been published in seven languages.

By the same author

The Sporting Club
Ninety-Two in the Shade
Panama
Nobody's Angel
Something to Be Desired
An Outside Chance: Essays on Sport
To Skin a Cat

The Bushwhacked Piano

Thomas McGuane

Minerva

A Minerva Paperback

THE BUSHWHACKED PIANO

First published in Great Britain 1989
by Mandarin Paperbacks
Michelin House, 81 Fulham Road, London SW3 6RB

Mandarin is an imprint of the Octopus Publishing Group
Copyright © 1971 by Thomas McGuane

British Library Cataloguing in Publication Data

McGuane, Thomas
  The bushwhacked piano.
  I. Title
  813'.54[F]

  ISBN 0-7493-9030-1

Printed in Great Britain by
Cox and Wyman Ltd, Reading, Berks.

This book is for
my mother and father.

When the sea was calm
   all ships alike
Showed mastership in floating.

            —W.S.

The Bushwhacked Piano

1

Years ago, a child in a tree with a small caliber rifle bushwhacked a piano through the open summer windows of a neighbor's living room. The child's name was Nicholas Payne.

Dragged from the tree by the piano's owner, his rifle smashed upon a rock and flung, he was held by the neck in the living room and obliged to view the piano point blank, to dig into its interior and see the cut strings, the splintered holes that let slender shafts of light ignite small circles of dark inside the piano.

"You have spoiled my piano."

The child would remember the great wing of the lid over his head, the darkness, the cut wires curling upon themselves, the smell of spice and the sudden idea that the piano had been sailed full of spice from the Indies free of the bullet holes that would have sent it to the bottom, resonant with uncut strings, its mahogany lid slicing the wind and sheltering a moist and fragrant cargo of spice.

What an idea.

After that, wisdom teeth, a perfect horror: one tooth

slipping out as easily as an orange seed popping from between your fingers; the other less simple, requiring the incision of a flap of skin and the chiseling through a snarl of impacted roots and nerves, the tooth coming away in splinters and his very mortality flashing from the infected maw.

Then: a visit to his grandfather's farmstead. Abandoned. The windows glinted blank on a hay field gone entirely to pigweed. Wingnuts made soft black moons in the punky wood of ruined shutters. When he shielded his eyes at the front porch window and saw into the old kitchen, he perceived the pipes of myriad disconnections, jutting and pointing into space; and, in the half-light of a far corner, a white enamel water heater, a rash of rust broken out on its sides, crouched like a monster. When he kicked in the front door, it swung wide and wobbling; its lock spilled screws far too long. He started to explore but quit at the bathroom where a tub poised lightly as a dancer on cast-iron lion's feet, its faucets dry, bulbous.

Years away but, he thought, in direct sequence, a woman sat on a blue stool striking at her hair with a tortoise-shell comb. And behind, on the bed, Nicholas Payne, her seducer, sighted between the first two toes of his right foot, wishing his leg were a Garand rifle.

There were any number of such things from that epoch, but a handful seemed to make a direct footpath to lunacy: a stockbroker's speckled face, for example, his soft, fat eyes and his utterly larval voice.

He was too young to have to make such connections, rolling across an empty early-morning city, red-eyed in an eggstained bathrobe, a finger in each corner of his mouth drawing it down to a grotesque whitening slit through which he pressed his tongue. Since they found him curiously menacing, the attendants supplied a canvas coat

12

with longish sleeves. It was insulting and unnecessary.

That was some time ago now, and he recovered at home. When he was being odd, he would sometimes, at night, go to his bedroom window, ungirdle, and urinate on the walnut trees radiant below him in the moonlight. Sometimes he boiled eggs on the electric range and forgot to eat them or went into the closet and stood in the dark among all the dusty shoes. He had an old cello, painted blue, and he often sawed upon it. One night he took the pliers to its strings and that was that.

His family said that he could not be trusted around a musical instrument.

Then, just when he was doing so well in school, he lit out on a motorcycle. And nowadays that trip would come to him in happy little versions and episodes. Anyone could see that he was going to pull something like that again. Even his mother's friend who had managed the Longines Symphonette could see he was fixing to pull something. She taught piano, and Payne took from her.

But all Payne could remember was that first cross-country trip. He was on an English Matchless motorcycle and headed for California. Nebraska seemed so empty he sometimes could scarcely tell he was in motion. Those were soil-bank days and you had to watch out for pheasants on the road. Payne felt intuitively that a single, mature rooster could disable an English racing machine. Later, he recalled two cowboys outside of Vernal, Utah, in a windstorm, chasing a five-dollar bill across a feed lot.

A girl rode with him from Lordsburg, Colorado, to Reno, Nevada, and bought him a one-pound jar of Floyd Collins Lilac Brilliantine to keep his hair in place on the bike.

And California at first sight was the sorry, beautiful

Golden West silliness and uproar of simplistic yellow hills with metal wind pumps, impossible highways to the brim of the earth, coastal cities, forests and pretty girls with their tails in the wind. A movie theater in Sacramento played *Mondo Freudo*.

In Oakland, he saw two slum children sword fighting on a slag heap. In Palo Alto, a puffy fop in bursting jodhpurs shouted from the door of a luxurious stable, *"My horse is soiled!"* While one chilly evening in Union Square he listened to a wild-eyed young woman declaim that she had seen delicate grandmothers raped by Kiwanis zombies, that she had seen Rotarian blackguards bludgeoning Easter bunnies in a coal cellar, that she had seen Irving Berlin buying an Orange Julius in Queens.

In the spring of that year, San Francisco was dark with swamis. He didn't stay long. Until that fall he lived north of San Francisco in a rented house, in the town of Bolinas. The memory of that now isolated these months to a single morning when he had turned out at dawn and gone to the window. Looking across the meadow that was the southern end of the low, vegetated mesa he lived upon, he could see the silver whale shape of fog that lay in from the sea, stilled, covering Bolinas, the lagoon and the far foothills. The eucalyptus around the house was fragrant in the early wet sun and full of birds. Firing up the motorcycle, he went spinning down Overlook Road toward the ocean rim of the mesa, straight toward the wall of fog at the cliff. Shy of the edge, he swung down onto Terrace Road and dropped quite fast through the eucalyptus and cedar, really as fast as he could go, through repetitive turns, the smells by-passing his nose to go directly to the lungs, the greenery overhead sifting and scattering shadows, the dips in the road cupping sunlight, the banked turns unfolding his shadow, the whole road flattening out, gliding along the base of the Little Mesa, down the corrugated concrete ramp onto the beach where he found himself in the fog with the sun melting it into streamers and the beach dark, streaked, delicately ridged like contour plowing; and everywhere the rock underpinning nosing through the sand and Payne obliged to steer a careful fast course with the front wheel swimming a little, until he reached Duxbury reef where he once caught a big, blushing octopus the color of any number of slightly gone-off tulips, as well as gunnysacks of monkeyface eels, cabezone and cockles— provender. He set about now getting mussels, snatching them off the rocks impatiently with less philosophical dedication to living off the land than to eating mussels at intervals of twice a week steamed in sixty cents a quart, third-press mountain white, and fennel. When he finished his work, he sat on the largest boulder at the end of the reef, the base of which was encircled with drifting kelp, weed and the pieces of a splintered hatch cover. The fog retreated to an almost circular perimeter within which a violet sun shone. The sea stood in a line of distant mercury. The sanderlings raced along the edge of the sea in almost fetid salt air. And Payne, thinking of home and knowing he would *go* home, saw with some concision that, as a citizen, he was not in the least solid. In a way, it was nice to know. Once he began to see himself as societal dead weight, a kind of energetic relaxation came over him and he no longer felt he was merely looking for trouble.

The homecoming itself was awash in vague remembered detail; the steamer dock on Sugar Island looked draped in rain. He remembered that. It was a wet, middling season in Michigan; he forgot which one. There were a number of them. And this: the condemned freighter *Maida* towed by tugs toward a chalky wafer of sun, toward the lead-white expanse of Detroit River, black gleaming derricks, slag—the whole, lurid panorama of cloacal American nature smarm debouching into Lake Erie where—when Payne was duck hunting—a turn of his oar against the bottom brought up a blue whirring nimbus of petroleum sludge and toxic, coagulant effluents the glad hand of national industry wants the kids to swim in. This was water that ran in veins. This was proud water that wouldn't mix. This was water whose currents drove the additives aloft in glossy pools and gay poison rainbows. This was water the walking upon of which scarcely made for a miracle.

Moping on an abandoned coal dock, Payne rehearsed his imagined home. He tried by main force to drag back the bass-filled waters he actually remembered. He dreamed up picturesque visions of long packed lawns planing to the river and the lake in a luminous haze beyond. He recollected freighters and steamers sailing by, the side-wheeled and crystal-windowed palaces of the D & C Line that had so recently gone in stately parade up the Canadian channel, the sound of their orchestras borne across the water to Grosse Ile.

But this time the *Maida* toiled before him on the septic flow, vivid with arrows of rust thrusting downward from dismal scuppers. On deck, a handful of men rather specifically rued the day. Life in the U.S.A. gizzard had changed. Only a clown could fail to notice.

So then, failing to notice would be a possibility. Consequently, he fell in love with a girl named Ann who interested herself in the arts, who was quite beautiful and wild; and who, as no other, was onto Payne and who, to an extent that did not diminish him, saw through Payne. In the beginning, theirs was one of those semichemical, tropistic encounters that seem so romantic in print or on film. Ann had a beautiful, sandy, easy and crotch-tightening voice;

16

and, responding to it, Payne had given her the whole works, smile after moronic smile, all those clean, gleaming, square, white teeth that could only be produced by a region which also produced a large quantity of grain, cereals and corn—and stopped her in her tracks to turn at this, this what? this *smiler*, his face corrugated with the idiocy of *desire* and the eclectic effects of transcontinental motorcycle windburn, a grin of keenness, blocky, brilliant, possibly deranged. And stared at him!

He went to her house. He croaked *be mine* from behind the rolled windows of his Hudson Hornet which in the face of her somewhat handsome establishment appeared intolerably shabby. He felt a strange tension form between his car and the house. The mint-green Hornet was no longer his joy. The stupid lurch of its paint-can pistons lacked an earlier charm. The car was now spiritually unequal to him. The wheel in his hands was far away, a Ferris wheel. The coarse fabric of the seats extended forever. All gauges: dead. The odometer stuttered its first repetition in 1953 when Payne was a child. A month ago he'd had a new carburetor installed. When he lifted the hood, it sickened him to see that bright tuber of fitted steel in the vague rusted engine surfaces. The offensive innocence of mushrooms. A thing like that takes over. A pale green spot on a loaf of bread is a fright wig inside of a week. These little contrasts unhinge those who see them. The contrast between his car and her house was doing that now. He could barely see through the windshield, but clear glass would have been unendurable. The world changed through these occlusions. Objects slid and jumped behind his windshield as he passed them. He knew exactly how a building would cross its expanse progressively then jump fifteen degrees by optical magic. Don't make me go in that house. Just at the center of the

17

windshield a bluish white line appeared like a tendril turning round itself downward and exploded in a perfect fetal lizard nourished by the capillaries that spread through the glass.

Gradually, he worked himself from the machine, went to the door, was admitted, went through to the back where Ann Fitzgerald was painting a white trellis and, paint brush in her right hand, dripping pale paint stars in the dirt. "Yes," she said, "I will." Indicating only that she would see him again. "Stay where you are," she said. An instant later she photographed him with a large, complex-looking camera. "That will be all," she smiled.

The steamer dock, the former property of the Sugar Island Amusement Company, defunct 1911, was a long balconied pier half-slumped under water. Near the foot of the pier, abandoned in the trees, was an evocative assortment of pavilions, ticket stands and stables. There were two carved and lofty ramps that mounted, forthright, into space. And the largest building, in the same style as the pavilion, was a roller rink. This building had come to be half-enveloped in forest.

It was nighttime and the ears of Nicholas Payne were filled with the roar of his roller-skated pursuit of the girl, Ann, at speed over the warped and undulant hardwood floor. He trailed slightly because he glided down the slopes in a crouch while she skated down; and so she stayed in front and they roared in a circle shuddering in and out of the light of the eight tall windows. Payne saw the moon stilled against the glass of one unbroken pane, gasped something like *watch me now* and skated more rapidly as the wooden sound sank deeper into his ears and the mirrored pillar that marked the center of the room glittered in the corner of his eye; he closed the distance until she was no longer cloudy and indefinite in the shifting light but brightly clear in front of him with the short pleatings of skirt curling close around the soft insides of thigh. And Payne in a bravura extension beyond his own abilities shot forward on one skate, one leg high behind him like a trick skater in a Dutch painting, reached far ahead of himself, swept his hand up a thigh and had her by the crotch. Then, for this instant's bliss, he bit the dust, hitting the floor with his nose dragging like a skeg, landing stretched out, chin resting straight forward and looking at the puffy, dreamy vacuity midway in her panties. Ann Fitzgerald, feet apart, sitting, ball-bearing wooden wheels still whirring, laughed to herself and to him and said, "You asshole."

2
_____

It was one of those days when life seemed little more than pounding sand down a rat hole. He went for a ride in his Hudson Hornet and got relief and satisfaction. For the time allowed, he was simply a motorist.

After the long time of going together and the mutual trust that had grown out of that time, Payne had occasion to realize that no mutual trust had grown out of the long time that they had gone together.

He had it on good evidence—a verified sighting—that Ann was seeing, that afternoon, an old intimate by the name of George Russell. There was an agreement covering that. It was small enough compensation for the fact that she had lit out for Europe with this bird only a year before, at a time when the mutual trust Payne imagined had grown up between them should have made it impossible to look at another man. Afterwards, between them, there had transpired months of visceral blurting that left them desolated but also, he thought, "still in love." Now, again, George Russell raised his well-groomed head. His Vitalis lay heavy upon the land.

The affair of Payne and Ann had been curious. They had seen each other morning, noon and night for the better part of quite some time. Her parents, Duke and Edna Fitzgerald, were social figments of the motor money; and they did not like Nicholas Payne one little bit. Duke said he was a horse who wasn't going to finish. Edna said he just didn't figure.

But Payne and Ann saw each other morning, noon and night. A certain amount of that time was inevitably spent up to no good. For Payne—and for Ann too—the whole thing seemed one of life's maniacal evocations, a dimensional reach-through, heaven.

Once, for instance, they were on Payne's little boat; he was in the cabin, adjusting the flame on the parabolic butane heater. Ann was on the bunk beside him, Payne in a Jesuitical hysteria of cross-purposes. Ann, clearly, prettily, waited for it. And Payne gave her one too, just like that. He looked underneath as he mounted her: a herring leaping from bank to bank, a marine idyll. Ann, for her part, should have never told him to hold on to his hat; because for an alarming instant he just couldn't get going at all. She patted him with encouragement and told him we were a big boy now. She slipped her ankles up behind his knees. Payne felt as though he were inflating, becoming a squeaking surface that enlarged getting harder and paler, a weather balloon rising through the stratosphere, merely a collapsed sack at the beginning, growing rounder and thinner with altitude, then the burst and long crazy fall to the ocean.

Afterwards they watched a Lake Erie sunset together; a bleached and watery sun eased itself down on the horizon and broke like a blister, seeping red light over the poison lake. They could count the seven stacks of the Edison Electric Company. They smelled with affection the effluents of Wyandotte Chemical. They slept in one another's arms on the colloidal, slightly radioactive swell.

Next day, he had a little hang-over. He smoked grass and consequently had the notion his chair was singing in a languid Dick Haymes voice. Outside, he was convinced the sky had been vulcanized. He tried to call Ann and got her mother who was cool to him. She reminded Payne that the whole family was packing to go to the ranch in Montana and that maybe it would be better if Payne called at the end of the summer.

Payne still could not believe that Ann would spend a minute with the other one. It broke his heart to think so. Her family hated him. She was always reluctant because of that to have him in the house at all. They knew he wasn't working. They had seen him on motorcycles and felt he had thrown his education away. Now, on the phone, Ann's porcine mother had it in her heart to tell him to wait until the end of summer to call. Payne doted on the pleasure it would bring to shoot the old cunt in the spine.

"Bartender," Payne said, "my glass is leaking." He looked at the flashing sign of the Pontchartrain Bar, visible from in here. "Have you ever tasted cormorant?"

He didn't know George Russell, the other, but he didn't hesitate to call him on the phone. "Listen George," he said, "I demand a cessation of stupidities on your part."

"Oh, Payne," George said with pity.

"I want to help you."

"Ah, Payne, please not that."

"I remember you said once George that you could not live without lapels."

"I didn't say that," said George with a debonair tone. *"I cannot live without lapels."*

"That's not true. Are you drunk or taking dope?"

"Whether it's true or not, why did you say it?"

"I didn't say it."

"What could it mean?"

"I didn't say it."

"What could that mean? 'I cannot live without lapels'?"

"Payne," George interrupted. "Can you live with this: Ann has been seeing me. Can you?" All Payne could remember about George was that he was what dentists call a mouthbreather. He had decent teeth which he had bought at an auction of Woodrow Wilson's effects. George hung up. Payne had one foot in the abyss.

Someone put some change in the jukebox. Two couples who knew each other materialized in a sentimental jitterbug. It was the kind of thing sailors did with each other and with brooms when they were brokenhearted on aircraft carriers in World War Two, flight deck jitterbugs with the kamikazes coming in for the coup de grace; it was the very dance a bosun's mate and a chief petty officer might have done a hundred and fifty-three miles out of Saipan with an eighty-five piece Navy orchestra playing Flatfoot Floogie on top of four hundred thousand tons of high explosives in a state of being approached by a religious Japanese in a bomb plane.

Payne headed back to his table, but some oddball had glommed it. "Who's the oddball?" he asked the bartender.

"You are."

"I saw a sign in the urinal that said 'Please do not eat the mints.' This goes for you." The bartender forced a laugh, throwing back his head so that Payne could examine the twin black ovals divided by the stem of his nose. He went to his table anyway, carrying a fresh whiskey. "Tell me about your family," he said to the oddball.

"Three of us is all," smiled the other, "two dogs and a snake." Payne looked at him, feeling his brain torque down into its first focus of the evening. The man picked up one of his galoshes from the floor and held it to his own ear. "I can hear Akron, Ohio," he announced. Payne was enthralled.

The man was sloppy and stretched-looking. Seeing Payne look, he boasted of having been most monstrously fat.

"Guess."

"Two hundred," Payne said.

"Close. Five years ago, I weighed four eighty. C. J. Clovis. You call me Jack." He pushed himself up. He was missing a leg. Then Payne saw the crutches. Clovis was neckless, not burly, and his head just sat in the soft puddle of his shoulders. "I lost more weight than I can lift!" He directed Payne's attention to the various malformations of his skeleton produced by the vanished weight. The hips were splayed, for example. "My feet went flat! I had varicose veins popping on me! Danger looked from every which way!" He told Payne about his two friends in the Upper Peninsula who both weighed over four hundred and who, like Clovis, were brokenhearted because at that weight they couldn't get any pussy. Therefore, they took a vow to lose all their excess. He dieted under the care of a doctor; his friends went on crashes of their own design. In the beginning he had reduced too fast and, consequently, as his body fed off itself, gave himself gout.

"Then I got this old fat man's disease, gangrene, and lost my leg."

"How long ago was this when you lost your . . . leg?"

"A month. But I'm going to get me an appliance and I'm as good as gold."

"They say a missing limb continues to hurt."

"Oh, naturally yes. Of an occasion."

"How did these other fat guys make out?"

"How did they make out?"

"I mean how did they reduce?"

"They reduced all right," said C. J. Clovis, looking angrily toward the bar.

"What do you mean?" Payne asked.

"They're dead!" Clovis looked around fidgeting, looked out the window and fidgeted furiously before looking back at Payne suddenly. "I'm going to get me some appliance!" His hands flew aloft like fat birds.

"I believe that you are, Jack."

"I'll be rockin and a rollin," he said with religious glee. "I'll be good as gold! I'll have a time! Do you understand, God damn it?"

". . . yes . . ."

"Stay a while and see me smile! Give me a chance and I'm gone to dance! I'll do the backover flip every trip! I'm gone to be reelin off the ceilin with a very happy feelin! *I'll be good as gold!*" Jack Clovis locked his eyes in position throughout the recital. Payne was locked in a paroxysm of embarrassment. "That is my pome," said Jack Clovis. "You take it or leave it."

"I'll take it."

"I could turn pro, Buster. You remember that." Being called Buster was the only part Payne didn't like.

"At what," he asked baldly.

"Why after I get that appliance I might take up an instrument. I could go a hundred different ways. You'll be able to hear me laughin a mile off and performin on some God damned instrument." He swung his head angrily through a hundred eight degree sweep. "When I think of them other two fat boys and what they're missing. Shoot! they too smarted themselves that time." Payne thought of the two fat boys ballooned against the insides of their coffins while his old friend schemed about an artificial limb, entirely magic in its pink plastic and elastic hinges.

The two men sat in a field of formica and did not speak. Payne could not accept the relief of an electric pinball machine that bloomed for him. Even without his gratitude, it spilled its pastel clouds and rang its bells while an unmoved player draped two fingers on the plunger and waited for it to get his victory out of its system.

"May I have your ear?" asked C. J. Clovis, a disturbing question from an amputee. "I need your confidence. You have heard haven't you of farmers who bring ten citrus fruits to bear from a single tree. You have heard of winter wheat. You have encountered, possibly, forced vegetables. I cannot go into it at this time; but let me say only this. There is a special application of these wonders that applies to the life of bats. And the potential? Top dollar. I will say no more.

"My own appliance," he continued to say, "which I mean to have in no time flat will be itself a natural wonder. I have confidence in it. It will have more actual articulations in it than a real limb. Though I will still be a monopod, this aluminum wonder will fetch me from spot to spot. Your name and address?" Payne gave it to him. "Let me drink in peace, sonny. And one last thing. Remember, won't you, that I am in the Yellow Pages."

"Yes, sir."

You do meet some people in a bar, thought Payne who continued drinking. Gradually, he ceased to think of the unimaginable C. J. Clovis; and to nurse, instead, his obsession with the possible infidelities of Ann. He thought of calling the house but knew his fears would be heard in his voice. He was, moreover, a little intimidated by her parents. They were good at their world at least; and he seemed bad even at his. Darling be mine I love you. More Black-Jack Daniels, he said, and make it snappy. I am the customer. It was brought. "I pay," he said lashing simoleons to the countertop. "I own a chain of wurlitzer chicken parlors and every Grade-A fryer has my brand on its ass." Later, some entirely theoretical argument with the bartender ensued during which the bartender thrust his face over the bar at Payne to inquire how anybody was going to wage trench warfare on the moon when every time you took a step you jumped forty feet in the air. Payne reeled into the night.

He was standing in front of the Fitzgeralds' door, in the dark, with no good in mind. Ann would be asleep. Inside of him, where all secrets were borne in darkness, a kind of Disneyland of the intestines went into operation, throwing forth illusions, mistimings and false alarums. Payne had a moment of terrible littleness. He pulled his sleeve back to learn the time and discovered he no longer owned a watch. He felt better. He saw again how he might be illustrious. The wrought brass knocker on the recessed oak door said FITZGERALD in stern, majuscule letters; above, heraldic devices worked in the metal itself proclaimed the Fitzgeralds rampant animals of one sort or another; while below—a pause while Payne goes completely out of focus, considers his mortality, our times and the music of the spheres, and refocuses—while below, then, a semicircle of smaller English uncials warned, *"Let Sleeping Dogs Lie."* It had been made to order, Payne surmised, by a microcephalic pump jockey from Burbank.

A stern Payne lifted the knocker as to announce himself, stopping on the upstroke. Its squeaking changed his mood. His thoughts were awash with all the noises he hated; especially Pomeranian dogs, wind chimes and windowpanes wailing under soft cloths. He lowered the knocker and released it.

Then he thought very hard. He stood without moving for a long moment and he thought quite as hard as he could. And when he had absolutely enough of that he turned the door knob slowly and firmly, opened the door, stepped inside and closed the door behind: a felon.

All of the lights were turned out on the first floor and in the living room, though there seemed to be light enough in the air for him to see his way; and crystal shone dully on the end tables. He wandered out of the living room and into the den, shutting the door behind.

In almost the first cabinet he rifled, he found brandy and the most magnificent Havana cigars he had ever seen, the legendary coronas, Ramon Allones Number One. His mouth was watering before he had one lit. With the first blue puff unraveling in the air, he poured himself a tall slug of brandy. He pulled Fitzgerald's Holland-and-Holland shotgun down from its cabinet, threw it up to his shoulder and, in his happiness, believed he saw the big canvasbacks coming in flat, slipping just under the wind and flaring all around him.

Could the Fitzgeralds have heard? Could they have heard him making shotgun noises with his mouth? Big ones? Like a twelve-gauge makes? He went to the door, stood behind it, pushed it open with his foot and jumped into the opening, brandishing the shotgun in the darkness. If anyone had been there, the situation had been clear and they had chosen not to show themselves. Payne pulled the door shut again and, holding the shotgun by the barrels, rested the butt on his shoulder and sat down, staring out of the dark window at the darker branches against it.

"Pleasure is not the absence of pain," he said aloud and swallowed all of the brandy. Instantly his eyes brimmed with tears and he ran around the room crying, "I'm dying, Egypt, dying!" Then he sat down again, took off his shoe, put the barrels of the Holland-and-Holland in his mouth and, sight unseen, pulled the trigger with his toe. There was a single, metallic, expensive and rather ceremonial English click. He took the barrels out of his mouth and thoughtfully replaced the cigar.

Feeling his way along with the shotgun, he began to explore the house. He went upstairs in the streaming moonlight. The first room on the right was a bathroom with a sunken tub and a shower nozzle on a pivoting arm. Payne unzipped his fly and began to urinate into the toilet, carefully shooting for the porcelain sides of the bowl. Then—and the gesture was perfectly aristocratic—he shifted his stream to the center of the bowl. It made a lot of noise. Then he flushed the toilet.

Payne tucked the end of the toilet paper in his back pocket, without detaching it from the roll, and returned to the hall. The paper quietly unwound behind him like a cave-explorer's twine. Over his shoulder, he could see its reassuring stripe in the darkness.

At the first bedroom door, he turned the knob. The door caught and would not open freely. He hesitated, then gave it a good jerk. It came free with a small creak. In the gaping space was an enormous double bed, Fitzgerald on his face, his wife on her back facing the ceiling. The enemy. It was some moments before he realized that the door was letting the wind pass through uninterrupted and the organdy curtains were standing into the room and fluttering and making noise. When he shut the door behind, he felt the unmistakable hum of fear. It had set up headquarters under his sternum. He lost track of what he was doing. His coordination departed and he made unnecessary noise with his feet. He still bravely managed to get to the edge of the bed and look down at the muzzle of the shotgun bobbing under Missus Fitzgerald's nose. He had occasion to recall the myriad exquisite ways she had found to make him uncomfortable. He remembered too—looking at her laid out like this—that Saint Francis Borgia had been impelled to his monkhood through horror at the sight of the corpse of Isabella of Portugal. Beside her, and invisible in a ledge of shadow, her husband rotated in the blankets and unveiled his wife. Wearing only a pair of floppy prizefighter's trunks labeled *Everlast,* her gruesome figure was revealed. It upset Payne to see such a thing. She began to stir then, and he withdrew the gun. In the moonlight, he could see where her nostrils had fogged its blue steel. The room was filled with cigar smoke now. Under Payne's eyes, the two Fitzgeralds blindly and in slow motion fought for the covers. She won and left him shivering and naked. He was as fuzzy and oddly shaped as a newborn ostrich.

A discovery that Ann was not in her room wrecked everything. Now the toilet paper, in snarls and strips forever, angered him. He thought balefully of climbing the old lady just to fix them; but felt, all in all, that he'd rather not. Free of the paper, he sauntered gloomily through the blue light tapping ashes on the rug, heartbroken. The bitch.

He bashed around the upstairs, not hearing the Fitzgeralds stir this time, and headed down to the den moaning a little. He poured another brandy, relit his cigar, gulped the brandy and smashed the glass against the far wall.

Finally, the throwing of light switches and the wily flap of carpet slippers came to his attention. A tongue of light advanced to the foot of the stairs. Payne scampered around the room repeatedly imagining he would get off with a spanking.

It was both of them. Payne was now crouched on the shelf beside the door. He turned at their sudden voices and rammed the gun cabinet door with his nose, actually slamming it. He knew paralysis. A voice: "Is this, is this, do they, where's the—?"

Then Missus Fitzgerald was in the den fixing instantly upon the smashed glass, the shotgun on the floor and the stain of brandy. Her eyes met those of Payne. Startled, she soon let her joy upon this ruin of him as a suitor be perceived.

"I'm a person you know," Payne claimed.

"Come."

"With valves."

"You're going to get a crack at cooling your heels in our admirable county jail," she said, moving toward him. "Do you know that?"

"I want my walking papers."

"No. You're going to jail you shabby, shabby boy."

"Back off now," Payne said, "or what I leave of your head won't draw flies at a raree show." He turned around and faced the bookshelves from five inches. "When I look I want you to have given me room to clear out. I'll count three." In the bookcases he saw, once he had focused at this close range, numerous volumes of interest, not the least of which was Borrow's incomparable *Lavengro*. But he was distracted by La Fitzgerald. By the time he turned and started out, she was screeching and hauling at the telephone. He wormed his way out of the narrow window into the garden; every pleached bush biting at once; dark, bark-packed, red meat bites all over him.

He went on all fours through the garden beds. He went, not like a man on his hands and knees, but with abrupt swinging motions of his limbs, head high for observation, hunting and on the move. This is the veldt, he thought, and this is how lions act.

I am leading the game, he thought, or not?

3

During the night, Payne frequently woke up, overtaken by horror. But nothing happened. He should have foreseen that. Not calling the cops was a precise piece of Fitzgerald snobbery. One's name in the papers.

He had breakfast with his mother who came in from an early round of golf. Her hair in a smart athletic twist, she flapped down driving gloves beside a robust ox-blood purse. Radiating cold outdoor air, she brought their breakfast to the porch. Today she was a lady eagle, Payne noted. She reached for a croissant with her modeled Gibson Girl hand.

They were able to watch the river from here. The table was surrounded by the telescope, bird books and freighter shipping codes with which Payne's father kept track of profitable tonnage on the river. ("There goes Monsanto Chemical loaded to the scuppers! They're making a fortune! Don't take my word for it, for God's sake! Read about it in *Barron's!*")

Through the top of the glass table at which they ate, Payne could see both of their feet splayed on the terrazzo.

He watched his mother probe daintily at her cheerless breakfast of champions awash in blue skimmed milk. And he knew by the warm detachment of her smile that she was about to spring something on him.

"What is it, Ma?"

Her smile soared up out of the wheat flakes, inscrutable and delicate. "You know Dad," her voice rich with inflections of toleration, of understanding. "You know how he is, well, on the subject of you doing something a tiny, well, the tiniest bit *reg*ular or res*pect*able, you know how he, how he, how he—

"I know but stop that."

"What?"

"How he, how he."

"How he wants you to simply take advantage of your most obvious advantages and join the firm; and it's not—"

"I will not subject myself to a career in lawr. I had my little taste of lawr in lawr skyewl."

"I see."

"Yass, lawr skyewl."

"Yes, well I do think you ought to know that if you repeat that speech to him—" She said this simply and very wisely. "—it would be useful to plan on your having your hash settled. Uh, but good, I'd say." She raised one thin arm emphatically, holding aloft her spoon; and a drop of milk, like a drop from the pale blue vein on her arm, quivered on the hand then ran into her palm. She turned her eyes to it. "You sneer at a man who offered to give you—"

"Strings."

"—to give you—"

"Too many strings attached."

"To give you, never mind, to hand over to you the finest law practice in the entire Downriver."

"Altogether too many strings attached to the finest lawr practice in the entire Downriver."

"But no—"

"But no I wanted to do something all by my lonesome possibly not even in the Downriver at all."

"Really, Nicholas, shut up, wouldn't you." Payne put a piece of hot glazed almond roll into his mouth and stopped talking. Maybe Duke Fitzgerald was hiring someone to kill him at this very minute and he was sending almond roll down a gullet that was doomed. He looked fondly on as his mother lifted her spoon again and dipped a chunk of bread and yolk from her egg cup.

"You think that your allowance is to be resumed."

"Okay, please, enough. I always supply my own funds."

"I couldn't go through it again," she went on doggedly. "Like last Fall. Your father working and you duck hunting every day of the week and filling our freezer with those vulgar birds. And the year before riding up and down the country on the motorcycle. It makes my head swim. Nicky, it makes my head swim!"

"I have to keep on the qui vive for spiritual opportunity."

"Oh, for God's sake."

"I do."

"And poor Ann. I sympathize with her and with her parents." Little do you know, Payne thought. I've got to bear down hereabouts.

"Mom," he inquired. "You want my motto? This is some more Latin."

"Let's hear it."

"Non serviam. Good, huh? My coat-of-arms shows a snake dragging his heels." His mother started giggling.

There was nobody here to make him see the world as a

mud bath in which it is right tough to keep showing a profit. He invented a joke to the effect that blood was always in the red and death was always in the black; and thought: What a great joke!

By the time his father got to him that evening, Payne, by careful examination, found himself adrift. The two men each had a drink in hand. His father had had his annual physical and was in an already exacerbated mood. He'd had a barium enema. If you had an intestinal impaction, he claimed, "that barium bastard would blow the son of a bitch loose." Payne said he would keep it in mind.

There had been trouble with the furnace. Since the house had been in his mother's family for four generations, that whole sector was implicated by the mechanical failings of the furnace. Mister Payne presently insisted that the machine had been salvaged from the English Channel where it had received the attentions of the German U-boat corps in 1917. "It was installed in our cellar with all its brass and corrosion intact and in its earliest glory. The touching ships' wheels by which the heat is adjusted have all seized in position so that the only real regulatory control we have is opening the doors and windows. I have been increasingly unamused during winter months in creating a false Springtime for six cubic acres around our house. The Socony Vacuum and Oil Corporation's fee for this extravaganza customarily runs to three thousand per diem."

"I understand how you feel," said Payne lamely.

"No you don't. I learned yesterday that the breakwater is sloughing at inconceivable speed into the river. I'm afraid if I don't pour a little concrete in there, we'll lose the pump house this winter."

Payne held his cold glass to his forehead. "I saw it was

crumbling myself." He crunched an ice cube; an illusion of his own teeth shattering.

"You don't realize the cost of these things," his father mentioned drily, his eyes leaden with authority.

"But if it has to be done."

"Of course it-has-to-be-done. But you regret the cost of it. The *cost* almost overshadows the *value* of the pump house you're trying to *save*."

Payne gave this a moment's quiet thought.

"Perhaps you'll let it go then," he said.

"*And lose the pump house! With an irreplaceable pump!*"

"Just what do you want me to say?"

"I want you to advise me. I would like to hear your ideas."

"Sell the house and buy an A-frame somewhere very far inland."

"Oh, well, if you're laying for something."

"How much sense does that make?"

"And maybe you ought to go easy on that stuff," said his father, lordly in the precision of his tailored livery. He jabbed a finger at Payne's drink, now splashing, then running, off the wall. "And if you don't want a drink, don't pour yourself one. The solution is not to pour yourself a drink and then throw the drink against the wall. It may be a solution in some circles; but it is not one I mean to finance."

"I bought this drink in a bar. I am its proprietor."

"I have attempted to talk about this breakwater, this ailing breakwater which, if it isn't healed, is going to drop my high-priced pump house into the Detroit River, irreplaceable pump, tightly built clapboard shed and all. I scarcely need mention that it will break your mother's heart. Her family has been in that joint for ten generations; and that pump house has borne witness to a hell of a lot of their hopes and fears. And I'll be God damned if I am going to play host to a squadron of union cowboys at six bucks apiece per hour just to keep the Detroit River out of the lawn and I suppose, ultimately, the basement."

"All right," Payne said, "I'll fix the breakwater."

"Don't do anything that's too rough for you."

"I've had enough hectoring now," Payne said. "I'll fix your breakwater but I've had enough of the other thing as of right now."

"You do as you wish, my boy." He gave the smile of love and understanding that is done primarily with the lower lip. "You have your life to live. Otherwise—"

"Other than what?" Payne interrupted, having become, some time ago, an expert on these lawyers' jumps by which a grip is obtained upon the testes, an upper hand as it were.

"Other than your performing some reasonable duties around here as a basis for our providing, gratis, your keep, I don't see how we can let you go on."

"You've muffed it now," Payne said. "I would have done it anyway. That's too bad."

"I've smiled through any number of months of your aimlessness, punctuated only by absurd voyages around the country in motorcycles and trash automobiles. I just find the Rand McNally approach to self-discovery a little misguided. I want you to know that I won't let you lie doggo around the house awaiting another one of your terrible brainstorms. My rather ordinary human response has been to resent having to go to work in the face of all that leisure. I, of course, stupidly imagined that this leisure has been not possible without my going to work. Once I had seen *that* I knew I could at least have the pleasure of being the boss. I know it's idle; but it gives me a cheap and real thrill."

"You make it pretty clear," said Payne with admiration.

"In other words," his father said pleasantly, "fix the breakwater or get out."

"Okay."

"Are you going to fix it?"

"Oh, not at all."

"You'll have to go," his father said, "you'll have to get out."

They strolled around. It was a pleasant evening and the garden beds smelled better than they would later on when they were grown over with summer vegetation.

The next morning, they talked in the driveway. Now his father's mind was on his briefs again. And the talk didn't please Payne as the one the day before had. His father, then, stood, hat in hand, bored to tears. "You're through here now," he said with muffled alarm. "Now what are you going to do? I mean . . . what? In terms of your education you're perfectly set up to . . ." His face looked heavy and inert as though you could have carved from eyebrows to chin and removed the whole thing without hitting bone. ". . . to . . ." He looked away and sighed, rotated the hat ninety degrees in his hand and looked at the door. ". . . you could . . ."

The boredom was infectious. "I could what?"

"I could find you a slot as a publicist."

"Non serviam," Payne said, "I've been reamed."

"What in God's name do you mean?"

"I actually don't have a clue."

They kissed like two Russians. "Goodbye."

The minute his father drove off, Payne's hemorrhoids

began hurting. The same thing preceded the last motorcycle trip, commencing with a gruesome fistula that fought eighty dollars worth of Cheyenne penicillin to a draw. Interminable Sitz baths in flimsy flophouse sinks had given him the legs of a miler. Payne knew the showdown was not far away.

Payne felt that he was wrong to always hang in to bitter ends. The current declining note was an instance. He had lived too long with all the irritants of life at home, small contestations and rivalries which inconvenienced his happiness pettily. A kind of drear mountainous persiflage always accompanied such encounters. He ended by being buried in the piss-ant social inclemencies which turned him into the petulant loafer par tremendoso he himself regretted being.

In the past, he had run up and down America unable to find that apocryphal country in any of its details. His adrenalin cortex spumed so much waste energy that a lot of amazing things happened. And he deliberately changed his highway persona day by day; so that, across the country, he was variously remembered for his natty dress, for his opposite of that, for his persistent collection of "data," for his arbitrary and cyclonic speechmaking, for his avowed devotion to his mother and father, for his regular bowel movements, for his handsome rather loosely organized mock-Magyar face, for his tiny library and transistorized machines locked away in ammunition tins, for his purported collection of the breakfast foods of yesteryear, and for his habitual parabolic coursing through the U.S.A. with attendant big trouble, pursuits and small treasured harbors of calm or strange affections along traveling salesman lines, facing enemies with billboard-size declarations of a dire personal animus, cluttering hundreds of small midland streets with regrettable verbs and nouns, sharp ones, heavy ones and ones which made barricades and tanktraps in peaceful summer villages where no one was asking for trouble.

In most ways it had been an awful strain, one he'd been glad to finish. Now, being on the verge of it again, he felt an uproarious tension in his mind.

4

People turn up.

For much too long, he continued to appear dazed. He often thought, "I couldn't have been more of a pig." Interested only in things that provided no morning after, he paid out deceptive conversations that made everyone in earshot fidget.

When he closed his eyes, Ann seemed to speed through a cobalt sky, a lovely decal on the rigid Ptolemaic dome. Every room gave at the corners. And why should anyone in the fat of late spring imagine that winter was not far away, scratching its balls in some gloomy thicket?

He dreamed and dreamed of his adolescence when he had spent his free time watching medical movies, carrying a revolver, and going around, for no reason, on crutches.

He was interested these days in how people listened.

He heard them. Completely buggy in the frame bed, he pawed the wall for the switch. They were down there: dogs. He climbed out of bed, driving a putty-colored shadow to the stairhead. At the bottom, a sea of fur flowed toward the toilet. He heard them taking turns drinking. He was excited and frightened. He felt a long, terrible oblong of space standing out from his chest and going all the way to the first floor.

The next day, he went to see a World Adventure Series movie of Arabia and talked for hours about Death In Africa. Two thousand years of desert heat turns a man's body into a weightless puffball which can be made into a useful kayak by slitting the paunch. Take it fishing. Show your friends.

He called Ann at the ranch. "Have you been arrested?" she inquired.

"Not yet."

"Oh, well. I didn't know what they were going to do."

"I'll never forget it, Ann."

"I wouldn't think so, no."

"I couldn't have been more of a pig."

". . . well . . ." she said equivocally.

"Things good there on the ranch?"

"There's this new foreman," Ann answered, "he's sort of beautiful and mean."

"I can handle myself," Payne said.

"You apparently thought so," Ann commented, "when you perched on the mantel that night—"

"On the shelf actually."

"—and screamed like a crow—like a crow—at mother. That's something, all in all, for a prize."

"I got one," Payne said mysteriously.

"Nicholas, oh . . ."

"You're crying."

"This call . . . is getting expensive."

"You are crying aren't you?"

". . . I . . ."

"I see you," Payne began clearly, "almost as a goddess, your hair streaming against the Northern Lights. And you tell me that this call is getting expensive. When there's a picture of you in my head which is an absolute classic. On the order of something A-1." In front of Payne's chin three holes: 5¢, 10¢, 25¢; a tiny plunger dreams of a plungette; glass on all four sides, circles of hair oil printed with a million hairlines and underneath, a tan-colored tray, scratched with names, a chain and a directory.

"Nicholas," Ann said, "try to train yourself to have a healthy mind."

"To what end?"

"Happiness and art."

"Oh my God." He concluded swiftly and hung up.

Hit the door and it folds. Fumes and automobiles. I've landed in a part of the American corpus that smells bad. The body politic has ringworm. These women. Really. All of them perfect double-headers. Smile at both ends. Janus. Make their own gravy like dogfood. I've been up against all kinds. Some of them lift an arm and there is the sharp- ishness of a decent European cheddar. And that art talk. I know what it leads to: more of her excesses in its name. And things like relinquishing underwear to protest the bugging of her phone by the CIA.

Appropriately, a hand-painted sign adorns an opposing brick wall: a weary Uncle Sam in red, white and blue stretches abject, imploring hands to the beholder; a reced- ing chin has dropped to reveal the mean declivity of his mouth, which says "I NEED A PICK ME UP." Payne ap- proached, saw with shock the signature: *C. J. Clovis Signs.* Back in the booth, he splashed through the Yellow Pages and found his name.

Fascinated, Payne started, seeing another, up the alley

which ended a quarter mile ahead with a blue gorgeous propane tank; the other end, a little white gap of dirty sky like the space between the end of a box-wrench held, for no reason at all, to the eye, a little space and, in the center, a red quaint telephone booth, where he had spoken. A radio played, its fell music contested by a rabid squabble of "electrical interference." Here was no scene for a happy boy. This was a land of rat wars, a dark fiefdom of bacteria, lance corporals with six arachnid legs.

The far wall, over the propane tank, between drain pipes spangled with oxidation, another sign, this depicting a dark Andalusian beauty, possibly a bit literal. Behind her the municipal skyline arises, tendrils and building pieces, in a total nastiness of habitat; the barest tips of her fingers, palpitant and patrician, rise barely over the lower frame; cheap day-glo letters proclaim her message: "My hosbin's frans dawn lok me percause I yam an Eespanidge voomans." The signature—ye gods!—C. J. Clovis. Beneath it, his marque, a naugahyde fleur-de-lys.

If Ann were here she would look at him, eyes reeling with meaning. She would never have seen the humor of the sign on the next building which showed five crudely drawn French poodles spelling out PILGRIM COUNTRY over a New England landscape in technicolor dogspew. How would she take the last picture Payne could find which showed a "farmer" attacking a "housewife" whom he has caught stealing, by moonlight, in his vegetable garden? Underneath, *"Here's a cucumber you won't forget!"*

Payne, agog, sped, by foot, away from the area; and ended sitting on a curb. The question was whether he had seen that stuff at all. That was the question, actually.

Cautiously, he returned to the telephone booth and called Clovis' number and listened in silence to a recorded message: "Hello, ah, hello, ah, hellowah thur, zat you, Bob, Marty, Jan, Edna, Dexter, Desmond, Desilu, Dee-Dee, Daryl, dogfight, fistfood . . ."

Payne was slipping.

To his credit, he asked himself, "Did I hear that?"

The sun fell far astern of the alleyway.

A tired rat picked its way among the remains of an innerspring mattress, determined to find The Way.

A dark brown elevator cable suspending a conventload of aging nuns in front of the fortieth-floor office of a Knights of Columbus dentist, popped one more microscopic strand in a thousand-foot shaft of blue dust light.

Certain soldiers took up their positions.

An engineer in Menlo Park pondered possible mailboxes of the future.

In the half-light of an office, a clerk had a typist; the landlord, spying from a maintenance closet, made his eyes ache in the not good light and thought he saw two Brillo pads fighting for a frankfurter.

"I don't claim to be a saint," Payne remarked.

One leg had gone lame, his pocket itched for his old heater, his old Hartford Equalizer.

Millions of sonorous, invisible piano wires caused the country to swing in stately, dolorous circles around the telephone booth. Payne felt it hum through the worn black handle of the folding door. The directory, with its thousandfold exponential referents, tapped with the secret life of the nation.

He went off now, thinking of Ann: impossible not to imagine himself and Ann in some cosmic twinning; they float on fleecy cumulo-nimbus, a montage of saints says: It is meet.

And, picturing himself against the high interiors of the Mountain West, he thought of old motorcycle excursions. He looked at the Hudson Hornet and asked, will it do?

5

The Hudson Hornet appears at the mouth of a long bend, a two-lane county road in the Pryor Mountains of Montana. Bare streaks in wooded country, glacial moraine, scree slides like lapping tongues, sage in the creek bottoms, aspen and cottonwood. Behind the lurching Hornet, a homemade wagon rumbles on four six-ply recaps from the factory of Firestone and Co. The wagon is the work of the driver, Nicholas Payne. With a bowed gypsy roof, the sides are screen with hardwood uprights. Inside are bedrolls, an ammunition tin filled with paperbacks, a stack of Django Reinhardt records, a cheap Japanese tape recorder; banging from side to side in the springless wagon, a sheepherder's stove seems to dominate everything; its pipe can be run up through an asbestos ring in the roof and an awning lowered to enclose the sides. There is a Winchester .22 for camp meat. There is a fishing rod.

Payne walked around Livingston, hands deep in pockets, head deep in thought, feet deep in the dark secrecy of boots. He went into Gogol's Ranchwear and Saddlery to try on footwear. He had no money but he wanted ideas. He felt if he could hit on the right boots, things would be better. His throat ached with the knowledge that it would not be impossible for him to run into Ann in this town.

"Howdy!" The salesman. Payne sat.

"Boots," he said.

"What you got in mind?"

"Not a thing other than boots."

"Okee doke."

"Can I charge them?"

"Live in town?"

"I sure do," Payne said.

"Then go to her," said the salesman. "Let's get you started here." He brought a pair of boots down from the display stand. He rested the heel of one in his left palm and supported its toe with the fingertips of his right hand. "Here's a number that sells real well here in Big Sky Country. It's all-American made from veal leather with that ole Buffalo Bill high stovepipe top. I can give you this boot in buff-ruff, natural kangaroo or antique gold—"

"No."

"No, what?"

"It is not right that a cowboy should dress up like a fruit."

"Now you listen to me. I just sold a pair of boots to a working cowboy in pink turtleskin and contrasting water buffalo wingtips."

"You don't have to get mad."

"I sold a pair of dual re-tan latigo leather Javelinas with peach vamps to a real man. And you tell me fruit."

"No one said you had to be a meanie about it."

"Okay, we drop it." The clerk insisted that they shake hands. "Let's get you into a pair."

"Now I want tennis shoes in mocha java."

"I thought you wanted boots."

"If I go barefoot will you tint my pinkies Antique Parmesan?"

"Sir."

"Yes?"

"Gogol's Ranchwear and Saddlery doesn't want your business."

Payne went to the front of the store, stepped up to the X-ray machine, flipped it on and put his eyes to the viewer. There was a handle at its side that controlled the pointer which Payne directed at the memento mori of his skeletal feet on a billiard-cloth green background. He suddenly saw how he would not live forever; and he wished to adjust his life before he died.

Payne took to his room and napped unhappily until evening. He woke up thinking of how he had camped one night on the Continental Divide and pissed with care into the Atlantic watershed. Now he wasn't sure he should have. He tried to imagine he was saying toodleoo to a declining snivelization; and howdy to a warwhoop intelligentsia of redskin possibility with Ann as a vague Cheyenne succubus—the complete buckskin treatment.

But under his window, attendants drifted in a Stonehenge of gas pumps. Fill er up! America seemed to say. A blue, gleaming shaft descended cleanly under the grease rack and a Toyota Corona shot off into the Montana night. Hey! Your Gold Bell Gift Stamps! Poised against the distant, visible mountains, the attendants stood by a rainbow undulance of Marfak.

All the windows were open to the cool high-altitude evening; under the blanket of his rented bed, Payne had the sudden conviction that he was locked in one of the umbral snotlockers of America. On the pine wall overhead, a Great Falls Beer calendar with Charles Remington reproductions of wolves, buffalo and lonesome cowpokes who tried to establish that with their used-up eyes and plumb-tuckered horses they were entitled to the continent. George Washington had tried the same thing: Throwing coins across a river, he had glommed America from the English. Payne could even understand how, in the early days, Indians, oriented to turkeys and pumpkins, were depleted by unfired blunderbusses, sailboats, maps. Just as Payne felt macadam and bank accounts depriving him of his paramour.

It had been, he felt, another migraine spring. He sat up and bit into an apple, a handsome, cold Northern Spy; blood on the white meat; teeth going bad; tartar; sign of the lower orders; drop them at the dentist; refurbish those now you.

Sleep.

C. J. Clovis, former fat man and entrepreneur of large scale "gadgets" of considerable cost and profit to himself, sat in his Dodge Motor Home, easing a clear lubricant into the bright steel nipple on the upper articulation of his appliance. He smiled admiringly at the machined bevels at its "knee" and saw the little quarter-arcs of ballbearing brighten with oil. Laced neatly to the aluminum foot, with its own argyle, a well-made blucher seemed quite at home.

The built-in television murmured before him: the Johnny Carson show. Clovis flicked it off and rolled out two blueprints on the dining table, weighting the corners with heavy coins of some foreign currency which he produced from his pockets. The plans depicted a model of a bat tower which Clovis would build for America; modern, total engineering of bat enclaves, toward a reduction of

51

noxious insects in the land. On the prints, the handsome-
ness of the structures was not hidden; they arose with loft-
iness from formed concrete piers and had stylish shake-
shingle roofs surmounting three tiers of perforations
through which the bats could enter. The floor plan, if that
is what it must be called, was based loosely on the great
temple of Mehantapec in the Guatemalan highlands. That
is, the "monks" in this case, bats, dwelt in individual but
linked sequences of cells roughly oblong in cross section,
each of which debouched into a central chute or shit-
scuttle; the accumulation, a valuable fertilizer, could be
sold to amortize the tower itself.

The bat tower involved sixteen hundred dollars in materials and labor. Clovis had slapped a price tag of eight
thou on the completed item; and considered himself
prepared to be beaten down to five. Not lower. Not in a
land where mosquitoes carried encephalitis. Next a note to
Payne who had been reamed and would not serve: offering
him a position as crew boss in an operation dealing in the
erection of certain pest control structures, a highly engi-
neered class of dealie. No holds barred financially. Need
aggressive young man with eye on main chance. Address
me Clovis/Batworks, poste restante, Farrow, North Dakota. All the best.

Clovis worked his way toward the stern and made himself a nightcap: eleven fingers of rye in a rootbeer mug,
and adjourned to the toilet for a rapid salvo; a fascinating
device, the machine used flame to destroy the excrement.
Clovis stood in now slow-witted eleven-finger wonder as
the little soldiers accepted the judgment of fire. Like
toasted marshmallows holding hands, they became simple
shadows and disappeared.

The instant before he fell asleep in the comfortable double bed, he commenced to feel sad. C. J. Clovis had every

right to believe, as he did, that it was no fun to be shaped like a corncrib under a tarpaulin and to have only one leg. He was already sick of the appliance. He looked out of the high laminated window to Sagittarius on the close night sky feeling the ache of tear ducts under his eyeballs; and thought, soon it will come. . . .

In the early morning, under Payne's window, no one moves at all. All along the curb, cars, pick-ups and stake trucks are angled in. The street is dusty in front of rolled awnings, conventional stores in a region where Montgomery Ward sells roping saddles. The Absarokas tower at the south end of Main Street; east of town a fish in whitewashed stones decorates a snuff-colored mountainside, its dorsal exaggerated where children walked too far with their rocks.

At this very moment, Payne should have been seeing Ann. Was it that he feared arrest?

Some time ago, when Payne and Ann had first met and been so interested in one another, Ann went to Spain with one George Russell, a young associate of her father's. She had in Ann Arbor developed a reaction to the ineffectual group of bridge-playing bohemians who hung around the Union and with whom she, as an *artiste*, spent her time. George, who at least seemed decisive as her new friend Payne did not, convinced her to make the trip. Unlike the bridge players, she thought, George was the kind who could receive and transfer power, big G.M. power. Nevertheless, her societal notions were such that she could, despite her infatuation with Payne, conduct a trial run for her European trip, with George, in a Detroit hotel. As far as Ann was concerned, it was just barely okay. George's fiscal acumen was not matched in his bedroom performances. He seemed weirdly unsuitable.

Parenthetically, it was Payne's upset that impelled his first cross-country motorcycle trip. Her departure made him reckless enough that he overworked the motorcycle and blew a primary chain outside Monroe, Michigan (home of George Armstrong Custer, who went West) at seventy miles an hour; and locked both wheels. He went into a long lazy succession of cosine curves before buying the farm altogether in a burst of dirt and asphalt followed by three shapely fountains of gravel; the last of which darkled the fallen cyclist's features for only a single instant of that year. No serious injury ensued; just a lot of mortifying road burn. Nine days later, he hightailed it for the Coast.

Thinking of Ann organized Payne's effort; any enlightenment proceeding from the present freedom of his condition, however irresponsible that freedom may have seemed, would finally devolve happily upon their connubial joys. He would tell her about all his wild days. He would tell her about his motorcycle in the mountains, the blue sheen of Utah glare ice when he rode down the west slope of the Uinta Mountains to fine snowless towns lurid with cold; about eating bloodwurst sandwiches for the three days he was camped in the Escalante Desert and up on the Aquarius Plateau. He would make little mention of the cutie he dogged repeatedly at the entrance of his Eddie Bauer nylon and polyvinyl expeditionary tent whose international burnt-orange signal color brought the attention of a big game hunter down in the timber who watched the fleering fuckery in his 8X32 Leitz Trinovids. The same girl who bought him the Floyd Collins Lilac Brilliantine to hold his hair down on the bike, showed him some American Space outside of Elko, Nevada, in the bushes near a railroad spur. She liked him to tell her he was a hundred-proof fool who was born standing up and talking back. It had been a beauty autumn with falcons jumping off fence posts like little suicides only to fly away; an autumn of Dunlop K70 racing tires surrounding chromium spokes that made small glittering starscapes in the night. "I'll take a car any day," she had said. "You cain't play the radio own this."

To see Ann now, well, never mind. I'm fundless. I want to be demeaned by postal money orders. Kiss me. I'm not one of your deadbeats.

A stake truck made a huge, pluming trail of dust coming West from the Boulder River. The dust washed out sideways on the scrub pine, rose high behind the truck and turned red in the early morning sun. Payne had nothing to play his Django Reinhardt records on.

He thought of the two of them becoming one and didn't like the idea. The shadow of the Waring Blender. Short of sheer conjugality, he didn't see why that would be any better than the billiard collisions that marked their erratic, years-long circling of one another.

If only he could see her. That was the thing. Not an idea. A thing of a certain weight. They would wander through the bones of an old buffalo jump, picking up flakes of jasper and obsidian, pausing now and again for that primordial rhumba known to all men. She would have a Victrola for his Django Reinhardt records. They would lurch and twitch from the dawnlit foothills to the sweet sunset-shattered finality of the high lonesome.

Held in abeyance, the question of Clovis, whose letter, queerly put, suggested to Payne a chance of productive movement, a set of brackets for this other. But to respond to Clovis' offer frightened him a little, like jumping a train, not for what it vouchsafed immediately; but for what it threatened in the long run. Once started, how stop? How does the foreman of a pest control project retire?

He wrote to Clovis and said, I'm your man; come get me. I have an operating radius of fifty miles, a need of: clean sheets, alcoholic beverages in reasonable quantities, harmless drugs, one Tek natural-bristle toothbrush with rubber gum massager, sufficient monies to clean or fix four pair Levis, four gaudy cowboy shirts, eight pair army socks, one Filson waterproof coat, one down-filled vest, one sleeping bag in the shape of a mummy, one pair Vibram-sole hiking boots, one pair Nocona Elegante boots with bulldogging heels and stovepipe tops, one scarf by Emilio Pucci, one pair artilleryman's mittens with independent triggerfinger and one After Six tuxedo.

He accepted, in other words, Clovis' offer with a sense that with the addition of this job to his routine, his life could be reconstituted like frozen orange juice.

Implacably, he would bring himself to Ann's attention in a way that reached beyond mere argument and calling of the police.

He would become a legend.

6

It is five o'clock in the morning of the Fourth of July on the fairgrounds at Livingston, Montana.

The day before, Payne sat in the grandstands in unholy fascination as Tony Haberer of Muleshoe, Texas, turned in a ride on a bucking horse that Payne felt was comparable to the perfect faenas of El Viti he had seen at the Plaza Mayor. One moment, stilled in his mind now, Haberer standing in the stirrups, the horse's head between his feet, the hind feet high over Haberer's head, Haberer's spine curved gracefully back from the waist, his left hand high in the air and as composed as the twenty-dollar Stetson straw at rest on his head: a series of these, sometimes reversed with the horse on its hind legs shimmying in the air, spurs making electric contact with the shoulders of the outlaw horse, then down, then up, then down until the time is blown from the judge's stand and the horse is arcing across the sand in a crazy gallop; a pick-up rider is alongside the bucking, lunatic animal, the bronc rider reaches arms to him and unseats himself, glides alongside the other horse—the outlaw bucking still in wild empty-saddle arcs by itself—and lands on his feet to: instant slow motion. Haberer crosses to the bronc chute with perfect composure; lanolin-treated goatskin gloves, one finger touches the brim up of the perfect pale Stetson with the towering crown; the shirt blouses elegantly in folds of bruised plum; faded overlong Levi's drop to scimitar boots that are clouded with inset leather butterflies. Payne sweats all over: *Make it me!*

But at five o'clock in the morning of the Fourth of July in the arena of the Livingston, Montana, fairgrounds, one day after Haberer rode, Payne crouched in a starting position in the calf chute. In the next chute, his quarter horse backed to the boards, Jim Dale Bohleen, a calf roper from the sandhills of West Nebraska, slid the honda up his rope and made a loop. He swung the loop two times around his head, flipped it forward in an elongated parabola and roped the front gate post; then, throwing a hump down the rope, he jumped the loop off the post, retrieved his rope, made his loop again, hung its circularity beside him with the back of the loop held tight under his elbow, leaned way forward over the saddle horn, his ass against the cantle and his spurs back alongside the flank strap. "Any time you are," he said to Payne.

Payne sprinted out of the calf chute, running zigzag across the graded dirt. Jim Dale gave him a headstart, then struck the quarter horse which came flat out from the chute, the rider rising forward, his looping rope already aloft for the moment it took to catch Payne, then darting out around Payne, tightening around his shoulders to an imperceptible instant as Jim Dale Bohleen dallied his end of the rope hard and fast around the saddle horn to flip Payne head over heels, the long thin rope making a gentle arc at the moment of impact, between the saddlehorn and Payne. The horse skidded to a stop and, backing very slightly to tighten the rope, dragged Payne. Jim Dale was upon him now, lashing hands and feet with his pigging string.

Payne lay there, feeling the grit between his lips and teeth. Beyond the judge's stand he saw the Absaroka Mountains, the snow in the high country, the long, traveling clouds snared on peaks. He remembered the record player over yesterday's loudspeaker—"I want to be a cowboy's sweetheart"—its needle jumping the grooves as six broncs kicked the timbers under the judge's stand to pieces.

"Two more," Jim Dale says, lazily coiling his rope between his hand and his elbow, "and I'll teach you how to work a bronc saddle." Payne heads for the calf chute.

The Fitzgeralds had box seats. They were almost the only rodeo patrons who were not in the grandstand and were consequently islanded among empty boxes. Mister, Missus and Ann Fitzgerald sat with Fitzgerald's foreman. He had been hired by the realtors who were managing the Fitzgerald ranch and keeping its books at a hefty fee. This was Wayne Codd. The ranch itself was one of a valleyload of write-offs, being sleepily amortized by the Bureau of Internal Revenue.

Wayne Codd was a young, darkly stupid man from Meeteetse, Wyoming. His eyes, small and close, suggested an alternative set of nostrils at the other end of his nose. It would not be fair to take unexplained peaks of Codd's recent history and evaluate him without talking of his past; it is possible, for example, that he was run over by an automobile quite a few times as an infant.

One of Codd's tricks was to drag his saddle out of the back of his GMC and take it into a bar where he would strap it on a stool, placed in the center of the dance floor, and make some little clerk sit in it all evening by slapping the piss out of him every time he tried to dismount. From time to time, Wayne Codd had been shot and stabbed with various weapons; but had not died.

Codd made no secret of his attitude toward the elder Fitzgeralds. He often said, *"Duuh!"* to Fitzgerald's obvious remarks and sometimes called him Mister Dude P. Greenhorn.

Nor did Codd hide his scratching lust for Ann. The Fitzgeralds had a little bathhouse near the stream from which their ranch was irrigated; and one day when he was supposed to have been repairing the headgate, Wayne Codd lay under its green pine floor, the interstices of whose boards allowed him a searing look at Ann's crotch. Two days later, he blew a week's salary on a Polaroid Swinger which he stored in an iceskate carrying case under the bathhouse.

It seemed to take so long to get through the drearier events. The barrel races, wild cow milking contests, synchronized group riding by local riding clubs often composed entirely of ranch ladies with super-fat asses, wouldn't stop. "Let's hear it for Wayne Ballard and his Flying White Clouds!" cried the announcer after a singularly fatuous event in which an underfed zootsuiter shot around the ring with his feet divided between two stout Arabians.

In the far towering Absarokas, a gopher and a rattlesnake faced off under an Engelmann's spruce. Mountain shadows, saturated with ultraviolet light, sifted forty miles down the slopes toward the Livingston fairgrounds. And far, far above this confrontation between two denizens of the ultramontane forest, a cosmonaut snoozed in negative gravity and had impure thoughts about a tart he met in Leningrad or Kiev, he forgot which.

"Folks," said the announcer mellifluously, "ah wont to speak to you about crooilty to animals. We have got the broncs coming up here in a minute or two. And as some of you good people already know, certain bleeding hort spatial intrust groups is claiming crooilty on this account. But I wont you good people to see it this way: If you wasn't watching these broncs here today, you'd be lickin the pore devils on some postage stamp." Far, far from the grandstands and box seats, the announcer raised hopeful hands to those who would see.

And announced the next six riders on the card.

The first was Chico Horvath of Pray, Montana. "Let's try the horse, cowboy! Yer prize money's awaitin!" Chico got himself bounced right badly and marred the stately cowboy's retreat with a slight forward bend from the waist indicating damage to the stomach. A clown ran out and collapsed in the dirt, jumped in and out of a barrel, frequently permitting his pants to fall down. Two good rides followed, in the order of their appearances, by Don Dimmock of Baker, Oregon, on a horse named Apache Sunrise, and Chuck Extra of Kaycee, Wyoming, on Nightmare. The fourth rider, Carl Tiffin of Two Dot, Montana, was trampled by a part-Morgan horse name of Preparation H. The fifth rider scratched.

"Our Number Six rider," went the announcement, "is a newcomer and an unusual one. Our cowboy is Nick Payne of Hong Kong, China. Nick spent his early years fighting Communism. Let's watch him now. He draws hisself a mean ole roan some of you know by reputation. Let's watch now, Nick Payne of Hong Kong, China, on Ambulance!"

"A Chinaman bronc buster," exclaimed Wayne Codd. "I have seen spooks and redskins but this here is some sort of topper." The Fitzgeralds, their interest galvanized, competed, clawing, for the binoculars. It was herself, La Fitzgerald, who confirmed their awfulest suspicions.

"It's him," she breathed. Ann raised her telephoto lens to the arena, her hand perspiring on its knurled black barrel.

Giddy with horror, Payne stood on the platform beside the Number Six bronc chute looking slightly down at Ambulance. He could not look straight at the horse. The ears of Ambulance lay back on his vicious banjo-shaped skull and the hoofs of Ambulance rang like gunshots on the timber. A man in a striped referee shirt—falsely suggesting that this was a sport we were dealing with here—ran up to Payne. "God damn it, cowboy! Get aboard!" Artfully, Payne avoided the nazzing of his undies. He looked down at his gloves. He moved as though underwater. Jim Dale had resined his gloves for him and they were sticky as beeswax. Looking, then, at Ambulance he wondered which of them was to end as glue. Everyone was yelling at him now. It was time. The strapped muscle of Ambulance's haunches kept jumping suddenly at the movement of hooves cracking invisibly against timber underneath.

He got on. Friendly hands from behind pulled his hat down so he wouldn't lose it. Payne tried to keep his legs free by extraordinary Yogic postures—inappropriate here at the rodeo—then dropped them into the stirrups and took his lumps. As Bohleen had shown him, Payne wrapped his gloved and resined hand palm up in the bucking rope. When the rope was wrapped to the swell of thumb, he closed his grip and mummified quietly. Then Payne lifted his left hand in the air where the judge could see it was free and clear.

Payne's joy—filling him now—was steady and expanding; and lit the faces of the cowboys sitting on the fences around him, smiling at one whose turn it was now, whose own million-color shirt filled and billowed softly in the wind, whose own sweet and gambling ass rested without deception on a four-hundred-dollar Association saddle having bought a one-way trip on a thousand pounds of crossbred viciousness. All questions of his history and ambition were null and void. Whoever it was had pulled his hat down around his ears would have known that. Payne had gotten on.

He nodded and said as the others had, "Let's try the horse." And someone reached down behind him and jerked the bucking cinch. The gate flew open and the cowboy from Hong Kong, confusing the clangor of the clown's comic cowbell with his own rattling testicles, wondered how, after two terrible plunging bucks, he had not only managed to stay aboard but also—as the horse soared forward onto its front legs so that he feared going butt first down over its head—had made the magic touch of spurs to shoulder, the left hand still sky-high and the right hand way back under his crotch somewhere.

Then the horse stood full length, towering on its satanic hind legs, wriggling and sunfishing its thousand-pound torso, and fell over backwards.

Payne cleared, rolling free of the enraged horse who, still on the ground, actually stretched to bite at him; its enormous legs churned on the opposite side of him as it surged to get to its feet again. Payne, already standing, his joy flooding in blinding rainbows that it was over before it had begun with no evidence that he could not ride a bronc revealed, adjusted his hat beside the flailing horse, took two exquisitely bored steps, kicked Ambulance a good one in the ass, turned and bowed delicately to the cheering crowd now rising to its feet in homage.

The horse finally got its footing and soared angrily away

between two pick-up riders, one of whom reached to snatch the bucking cinch free so that the horse seemed to glide to a stop, flaring at shapes and fences.

Payne smiled to the lingering applause and beat the dust from his Levi's with the borrowed Stetson straw.

7

Wayne Codd drove. Fitzgerald sat in front, not thinking of Payne. He was trying to imagine why all those polled Herefords he bought had calves with horns. He was suspicious that Codd, who had arranged the purchase, had just dehorned a lot of cheapjack range stock and turned himself a tidy sum. It was mortifying to think this throwback could have cheated him.

Ann sat in back with her mother. She burned with love and admiration while her mother merely burned. The four of them rode up the valley of the Shields and stopped when a shepherd drove his band of blackface sheep across the road in a single surge, his two dogs running importantly around their perimeter like satellites.

"You are to be strictly unavailable," counseled the mother in no uncertain terms.

Ann did not answer. She was finding it difficult not to respond to Payne's heroic performance. She still saw him insouciant far across the arena and beneath the judge's stand, a giant, vicious horse soaring over his head. It was too bad, she thought, that she lacked the nerve to call him, if only in her heart, Pecos Bill. It seemed for once his confusions and indecision were invisible and gone as he stood in perfect clear air under mountains—at one with the situation. And this made her think of his refusal to read her favorite D. H. Lawrence novels because he said Lawrence always tried to be "at one" with things.

"We weren't born in a Waring Blender," he told Ann. He called Lawrence "Lozenge" and frequently associated him with devices that made pulp from vegetables.

To the immediate east of them, in the Crazy Mountains, a Forest Service plane stocked a mountain lake with trout, releasing its cloud of fish against the Delft-blue sky.

Ann lay her head back on the tan leather of the Mercedes' seat and did quadratic equations in her head for a while; then rehearsed the skeletal articulations of the Rhesus monkey that she had dissected against Gray's Anatomy. For reasons only she knew completely, Ann was ready for ficky-fick.

Wayne Codd, two years on the job, had certain reservations about his employers. His predecessor as foreman had blown a ventricle and died the previous winter pushing bales of winter feed off the wagon. Codd thought the man was a good old boy and when his request of the Fitzgeralds—that he be buried on the old ranch—was *refused,* Codd signed off on them for good. The foreman had wanted his spot under the big sky, up on the old Soda Butte where he could see the ghosts of retreating Shoshone. Codd, then just a hand, knew he would succeed the old foreman so long as he didn't offend the realtors who were running the place; but the advancement embittered him. It still seemed that—even though the old boy had only worked on the ranch five-and-a-half weeks—his request to be buried up in the high lonesome deserved better than the Fitzgeralds gave him.

Instead, they sent the foreman's body back to the wife and child he had deserted in Wyandotte, Michigan. His union local buried him in his arc-welder's uniform. The casket was draped with leis. The funeral dinner was catered by River Rouge Polynesian Gardens.

Wayne Codd had not only the physical features but the memory of an elephant. He knew that when the chips were down the Fitzgeralds would go South on everything he damn well knew was decent. And that went for Ann. That is why, on hot swimming days, he put in the long, long hours under the bathhouse. At the end of the day, the little Polaroid Swinger seemed to weigh a ton; and for this trouble and the trouble of lying on his back swatting the big striped horseflies, his Stetson dropped over the pointed toe of one boot and the circles of honest cowpoke sweat expanding toward the pearly diamond buttons, he got a handful of obscure little photos of what looked like a field mouse behind bars.

Missus Fitzgerald stared at the first of their own sections, her mood utterly forged by the appearance of Pecos Bill. She had learned to identify the reddish furze of mature cheat grass and had been informed that it would not feed the stock. And though it was the only grass she could identify besides Kentucky Blue, she seemed to be singling it out of some fabulous variety when she cried, "That cheat grass!"

The ranch house, with its downstairs sleeping porch that gave the effect of a lantern jaw, was surrounded by lesser buildings, all log: the barn, stable, bunkhouse and shop. She could see it now at the end of the ungraded road in the cottonwood trees she considered neither here nor there. She was an enthusiastic bird watcher with a mild specialty in warblers. Out here, all the beastly birds of prey that appeared in her Zeiss weighed down her spirits. In fact, she had asked Codd over and over to shoot a big harrier, a marsh hawk, that she could see from the breakfast room, sailing low over the gullies and pockets. From time to time, Codd would blaze away to no avail. And Missus Fitzgerald, seeing the great hawk, felt anew that Nature was diminished by it. It was warblers she wanted, the little pretties.

They drove up front and parked. Fitzgerald looked around at the house and the yard. He looked at the great sheltering willow that had gotten its roots into the septic tank and gone beserk. "Peace," said Dad Fitzgerald. "Ain't it wonderful?"

The Fitzgeralds' Double Tepee Ranch, whose twin triangle brand aroused local cowboys to call it wishfully the Squaw Tits, sat on a bench of fat bottom land in a bend of the Shields River somewhere between Bangtail Creek and Crazyhead Creek. It was one of the many big holdings whose sale was consummated through the pages of the *Wall Street Journal*. The ranch had been founded, under its present name, by Ansel Brayton, a drover from New Mexico who had brought the earliest herds this far north. It was sold—through the *Wall Street Journal*—by Ansel Brayton's grandson, a well-known Hialeah faggot.

Fitzgerald was proud of his place and often said to his wife, "The ranch is good, Edna." He would stroll along the willows of his river frontage or along the lane of Lombardy poplars, stop beside the lush irrigated hayfields now mowed and raked, with the bales still lying in the combed golden order of the harvested acreage. It was his ranch, not Edna's.

Of course, she wanted as small a part of it as she could. From his G.M. earnings he had set up separate investment facilities for the two of them; and it produced a little happy contention. She had built, with her share, a wig bank on Woodward Avenue for the storage of hairpieces in up-to-date, sanitary conditions. She often compared its profitable records with the slightly scary losses of the Double Tepee. Fitzgerald had visited his wife's operation, walking through the ultraviolet vaults filled from floor to ceiling with disinfected hairpieces. It was not the Mountain West in there. Stunted workmen in pale green uniforms wheeled stainless wagons of billowing human hair down sloping corridors. Prototypes of wig style rested on undetailed plastic heads. No sirree, Bob, thought Fitzgerald, I'll take Montana.

The living room of the ranch house was two stories high with a balcony at the second story. It was all done in a kind of rustic art nouveau: birchbark ormulu and decorated extravaganzas of unpeeled log.

At the north end of the first floor was the library where they held today's meeting. The question at hand was whether or not to call the police. "I don't know," said Missus Fitzgerald, "any use of the police at all downgrades everyone involved."

"They are merely a facility."

"But they mean something tacky," she said.

"They are a simple public facility."

"I know what a public facility is," she said.

"Okay, all right." He waved her off with both hands.

"It's as if something low—"

"We pay for them. We ought to use them."

"Something shabby—"

In 1929 the Fitzgeralds were married. On their first morning together, he bellowed for his breakfast. She called the police on him.

"—merely—"

"—even vulgar or—"

He never asked for his breakfast again. Not like that. Sometimes he got it anyway, in those early days. Now the maids brought it. He bellowed at them, like in 1929. Let them try the law.

"Call the police," said Fitzgerald doggedly. "Tell them the circumstances. They'll hand Payne his walking papers so fast. Or I'll get the bugger on the phone myself. I'll tell him he just doesn't figure. Do you read me?"

In 1929, when two large bozos of the police profession snatched the up-and-coming economist from his breakfast table, he had doubts about the future of his marriage. As the shadow of his struggling form left a bowl of Instant Ralston in uneaten solitude, a vacuum fell between them that later became tiny but never disappeared. "The year of the crash," he often said wryly, meaning his own little avalanche.

Missus Fitzgerald had lost her rancor, temporarily, in the realization that Payne's inroads had been made possible by a certain amount of cooperation if not actual encouragement from Ann. It was so dispiriting. A pastiche of lurid evidence made it clear what she had been up to. Infamy and disgrace seemed momentary possibilities. And though she took a certain comfort from such abstractions, there were dark times when she saw an exaggerated reality in her mind's eye of Payne hitching in naked fury over her spread-eagled daughter or worse, the opposite of that. At those times, Missus Fitzgerald scarfed tranquilizers

70

again and again until all she could think of was heavy machinery lumbering in vast clay pits.

Fitzgerald was thinking he should have slapped the piss out of her in 1929, that rare crazy year. (Sixteen years before Payne was born when his mother and father were touring Wales in a rented three-wheel Morgan; and twenty years before Ann was born. Ann was conceived in 1948. Her mother, already Rubensian, to be generous about it, stood on an Early American cobbler's bench grasping her ankles as the then-wasplike Dad Fitzgerald— so recently the squash champion of the D.A.C.—laced into her from the rear. As he had his orgasm, he commenced making the hamster noises that lay at the bottom of his wife's subsequent sexual malaise. His legs buckled and he fell to the floor and dislocated his shoulder. What neither of them knew as they drove to the hospital was that Ann's first cell had divided and begun hurtling through time in a collision course with Nicholas Payne, then knuckling around the inside of a Wyandotte playpen.) But he never did and now it was too late.

"You wonder about old man Payne," said Fitzgerald.

"Yes, you do."

"He has the finest law practice in the entire Downriver."

"Yes he has."

"He's right up there, you know, *up* there, and he throws this classic second generation monstrosity on the world."

"You wonder about the mother," said Missus Fiztzgerald. "She was once the chairman of the Saturday Musicale. She got the Schwann catalogues sent to everybody. How could decent people develop a person in this vein? I ask myself these things."

"Yes, but like all women you fail to come up with answers."

"All right now."

Dad made his fingers open and close like a blabbing mouth.

"I'm sick of the theory approach to bad news," he said. "I'm a pragmatist. In my sophomore year in college two things happened to me. One, I took up pipe smoking. Two, I became a pragmatist."

Mom Fitzgerald began to circle the Dad, her neck shortening under the blue cloud of 'do. "Well, you little pipe-smoking pragmatic G.M. executive you," she said. The hands which banished bad thoughts flew about in front of her. "You're going to give us one of your little wind-ups, are you? Your college history, are you?"

"I—"

"I'll pragmatize you, you wheezing G.M. cretin."

"Your pills, Edna, your pills. You're getting balmy."

"Show me that little trick with your hand, where it tells me I'm talking too much."

"Get your pills, Edna."

"Go on, show it to me."

He showed her the blabbing motion with his hand at the same time he told her, "Get the pills, Edna." She slapped his hand open. He made the blabbing motion again. "Get your pills I said!" Then she nailed him in the blaring red mug and ran for it. He galloped after her grunting and baying as he hauled her away from the desk. She turned then and raked his chest with a handful of ballpoint pens and a protractor.

He tore open his shirt, revealing his chest, and seeing with his own starting eyes the blue and red lines all over it.

"You maniac! You shitbird! Oh my God you piss-face you!"

Wayne Codd, deliriously attracted to this compromising episode, sprinted across the immense living room. "Is there anything I can do?" he asked, looking in on the extraordinary uproar of Dad Fitzgerald stripped to the waist, his wife sobbing on the couch, her bum in view, sheathed in a vast reinforcement of pink rubberized girdle and a systematic panoply of attachments; everywhere it was not held back, terrible waffles of flesh started forward. Codd felt he had them dead to rights.

"Saddle my horse, Codd," said Fitzgerald.

"You want to ride horseback?"

"Saddle that horse you God damn mountain bonehead."

Codd looked at the scrimshaw on Fitzgerald's chest.

"No one talks to me that way, Fitzgerald."

"Oh, of course they do. Now saddle the horse. No cheap talk."

Codd darted for the stable. It was the wrong time for a face-off. He meant to keep a low silhouette.

Fitzgerald turned to Edna.

"Duke," she said. His chin rested fondly on his abstract expressionist chest. Their obsession with Payne was temporarily suspended in a vision of Instant Ralston, cobbler's benches and happy squash tournaments at a time when Europe was beating its way into the Stone Age.

"Edna," he said.

8

Ann troweled around the strawberry sets in her little garden, weighting the corners of each square of net. Sweet Wayne Codd had made her a little irrigating system, a miniature of those in the hayfield with its own little head gate and little canvas dam and little side ditches that went down all the little rows between the little strawberries. Each day Wayne came down and opened the gate, flooding the little garden with clear cold creek water that made the strawberries grow fast as wildfire. How sweet they would be too, she thought, bathed in mountain sunlight and floating in that heavy cream Wayne skimmed and brought up from the barn. Nicholas, are you thinking of my little strawberry garden?

Mister Fitzgerald rode his strawberry roan across the creek, his chest stinging with strawberry-colored tincture of merthiolate. He was on the lookout. He thought of all the sauce the old broad still had in her.

> ". . . what those five feet could do
> has anybody seen my . . ."

Payne towed the wagon up Bangtail Creek and, in an agony from his labors, sat waist deep in his sleeping bag. He leaned over to look at the vast strawberry evanescence that was ending the day and yelled at the sky, "I've had more heartaches than Carter's got little liver pills!"

Ann fluttered around her room in her nighty like a moth. It had come to be time to think again about George Russell. She had after all lived with this bird; and in the face of Payne's luminous appearance the day before, it seemed well to review the options. She transported herself to a day on which they had traveled through reasonably intact swatches of Provence, rolling along conspicuous in their Opel sedan among the pie-plate Deux Chevaux. There were the usual laments about American towns not having trees like that; and, withal, a pinched whininess was their sole response to all that was demanded by towns accreted upon Roman ruins. That day they reached the border town of Irun where, over the questions of Spanish border officials and views of the varnished heads of the Guardia Civil, they gazed upon the gray-green wonder-mass of España.

Through the efficiency of the crafty young executive, George Russell, they found themselves at the bullfights in Malaga, a mere day later. Ann's knowledge of that came in pulses, there in the window over the garden, the garden in Montana:

They watched the bullfighter set up the bull for the kill. The bulk of the fight—the queening and prancing—was behind them now. He put away the wooden sword and took the steel one and moved the bull with the cape to uncross his front feet. George beside her had been giving the most relentless play by play: The bull's tongue was out

because the picadors had stayed in too long and had pic-
ed the bull too far back. The placing of the sticks, George
said, had been arrant dancing. The torero's ringmanship
had been questionable; he had allowed the fight to continue until the bull's head lolled.

"Nevertheless," George summarized, "everything with
the right hand, and I'm thinking especially of the *derecha-
zos,* has been worth the trouble of getting here." Ann
nodded and looked back down onto the sand; at once, de-
pressed.

The bullfighter had folded the muleta over the sword,
reached out placing the cloth before the bull and, withdrawing the sword, rose up onto the fronts of his feet
sighting down the blade. The exhausted animal remained
fixed on the muleta. A moment later, it lifted its head from
the cloth and the torero stabbed him in the nose to drive
the head down. You can bet it worked. Ann looked away.
Even art . . .

"Listen to those English," said George. "The bastards
are cheering the bull!" The bullfighter went in. The bull
made no attempt to charge him. The sword went all the
way to its hilt and the bull did not fall over dead. Instead,
he turned slowly from where he had taken the sword and
began to walk away from the torero. He had his head
stretched out low and far in front of himself, close to the
ground. Part of the retinue joined the torero following the
bull in its circling of the ring. The bull walked in agony,
an ox driving a mill, the torero behind, patient, trailing the
sword in the sand. The bull stopped and the torero and his
retinue stopped as well. The bull heaved and vomited several gallons of bright blood on the sand and began plod-
ding along again. Presently, the hind legs quit and the bull
went down on its rear. The torero walked around in front
of it and waited for the completion of its dying. The bull

lifted its head and bawled and bawled as though in sudden remembrance of its calfhood.

Laughter broke out in the stands.

Then the bull just died, driving the one horn into the sand. The torero stretched an arm over his head in much the same gesture Payne had made in the bronc chute, and turned slowly in his tracks to the applause.

"C-plus," George Russell said. "An ear."

By then, anyway, it was not so easy to sleep. They had been in Spain some weeks now in the small house in the villa district of Malaga's North End: Monte de Sancha. The days were not hot but still clear and the nighttime came prettily, zig-zagging up the sloped system of streets and passages. And when it was dark it would be quiet for a few hours. By midnight, however, the high-powered cars on the coast road would begin their howling at almost rhythmic intervals, now and again interrupted by the independent screams of the Italian machinery, the Ferraris and Maseratis.

George, the employee of General Motors, and guarded car snob, dismissed the "greaseball hotrods"; but often paused in Torremolinos and Fuengirola to caress the voluptuous tinted metal or smile dimly into the faces of the drivers. Ann imagined the noise made him sleep even better; and in fact, coming in from the terrace, a sleepless middle of the night, the long cones of light pushed along beneath the house by a wall of noise rising and falling in sharp slivering of sound as the cars jockeyed for turn positions on the way to Valencia and Almeria, Gibraltar and Cadiz, she would see George, asleep on the big bed, his lip neatly retracted over the Woodrow Wilson teeth in something altogether like a smile.

That day they returned from Seville where George had

77

taken four hundred and nineteen photographs of Diego Puerta killing three Domecq bulls which he dismissed as brave but "smallish."

"Small but bravish?"

"Brave but smallish, I said."

"Then why do you take their pictures."

"Oh, come on."

She had seen in George an unusual, even troubling, interest in the bullfighters, passed off with the same misleading sneer as the greaseball hotrods; but once she had caught him pinching his hair behind between thumb and forefinger, looking at himself sideways in the mirror, and she knew he wondered how it would be to wear the bullfighter's pigtail—even in the clip-on version of the modern "swords"—and cruise the Costa del Sol in his Italian automeringue all the way from Malaga to Marbella where sleek former Nazis teased the flesh on the sun-dappled concrete of the Spanish Mediterranean and sent cards to Generalissimo Francisco Franco on his birthday.

With none of this to endure, the sight alone of George throwing the absolutely limp and filthy wads of Spanish bills at waiters, at the African who bent iron reinforcing rods with his teeth in front of the Cafe España, or at the concierge of the Plaza de Toros in Seville whose undershirted laborer son came to the door inopportunely as George highhandedly tried to bribe the mother; so that George very nearly got it, then and there, just got it; and when at the bars he would say in a loud voice, "Another Ciento Three para me," she would begin vainly to plot her escape and was only stopped when she could not think of any place she wanted to go. Sometimes, too, she stayed because she felt that suffering was good for an artist, the source of his wisdom.

So, then, ever since the grave of Cristobal Colon, and intermittently before, her escape had been to think of Payne. She could not, in her thoughts even, avoid the very beastly and useless things he did. But somehow the thought of his bad drinking, the spilling train of cigar ash always on his front, the ardent nonsense and volcanic cascade of lies and treachery, seemed now, as it had not when the two had been side by side to compare, unobjectionable next to George's calculations.

George was planning another trip now. Starting in Sicily they were going to follow thermoclines all worked out on a thin pad of tissue maps so that they would stay at a temperature and humidity least likely to rouse George's sinuses. Only the scenery would change.

But George was everybody's dream. Once her father and George were talking in the den and Ann listened in.

"How are they treating you at G.M.?" her father had asked.

"Oh, God," George grinned.

"That's a boy!"

"Trying to work me to death," George allowed.

"You ought to know why!"

"Trying to do five jobs at once. They think I'm—"

"You're going to go, George! You're going to go big!"

"—think I'm *atomic powered* or some damn thing."

"*Atomic powered!* Oh, God kid, you're gonna go."

Unable to think of it any more, Ann went out onto the terrace in the dark. Overhead, the standard decal moon of Spain hung under the auspices of the Falange. Under such circumstances, it was scarcely a bustle of nard.

She had fallen in love with Payne; or at least with the idea of that.

· ·

Payne dozed achily in his wagon, the roar of Bangtail Creek nearby. When Ann had come home from Europe she found Payne crazy. They rented a little house for a week. And stayed together.

Payne dozed and woke in completely unspecific exhaustion. Every night the dogs had come into the house. He knew they were down there. He always knew. He watched them for months. He looked for heads but could only see a glitter of eyes in his penlight. He never knew their number. He was not afraid. He let them drink from his toilet. He kept it clean for them. He left food but they wouldn't take it. He was never afraid. One week. She stayed and saw them. She held the penlight and they both saw them. They figured twelve feet and they divided that into four dogs. It could have been three dogs. They thought with terror that it could have been two dogs. Sometimes they giggled and talked about it being one dog. They heard them drink. They didn't know. It made them fastidious about the toilet. They didn't forget to flush in times like that. They knew the dogs were coming. They kept it clean. They made love and talked about the dogs. Payne was trying to put his suspension system back in order. For quite a while there it was okay. He needed to get in touch there again though. It was like some kind of middle ear trouble. He woke up and couldn't tell which way he was pointing, whether it was his head or his feet that were pointing toward the door. When the dogs came he would really start whirling. Maybe he should have shooed them out. He didn't see the point of that. Neither did Ann. He was awfully crossed up and the dogs didn't hurt and later Ann said that there had not been any dogs. He was fielding grounders. It had been hot all day. He imagined that all the leaves had turned.

That everything outside was bright with frost. That winter was not far away. He did not know about that. It wasn't that he wanted winter. He wanted to get his white Christmases off a bank calendar.

"It's all in your head," Ann said. Which was exactly right. Not that anyone was ever helped by that kind of idle information. But she tried so hard, so awfully hard. No she didn't. She didn't try all that hard. She always nailed him with that fucking Art. What Gauguin did. What Dostoyevsky did. What Lozenge did. He told Ann everything. True and false. She showed a preference for the false. He told her stories of Grandma making mincemeat in the late autumn up in Alberta with her great tallow-colored buttocks showing through her shabby frock. It was all false, all untrue, all gratuitous. She made a whole view of him out of it. A whole history. A whole artistic story of his childhood.

Then Ann began to catch up. She saw he had invented himself *ab ovo*. She was upset. After the first chink, he pissed away everything. She called him a mirage. That was the end of their week. She really laced into him. Underhanded stuff. Subliminal broadsides. But the mirage business hurt his feelings. There were certain areas where he was not a mirage. Period. There were certain areas where he was implacable, don't you know.

He kicked her out. Ann found out he was not a mirage in a way that brought her up short rather fast. Irony of being kicked out of the house by a mirage. He liked that sense of things. The recoil factor of reality. Now he couldn't see it. That kind of impatience. But he had been pressed. Two years of the most needle-nosed harassment from home.

Ten days later he saw her. A high-school science exhibit. He remembered it exactly. Ann was there. Right where they could see each other. There was a glass-enclosed diorama against the wall. It was supposed to be Patagonia. He remembered one tree full of plaster fruit. Looked like grenades. Hanging over everything on these thousands of fine wires was a cloud of blue parakeets. He left without a word. The most overweening cheap kind of pride. Not speaking. He would pay.

A false spring night. He was out in the garden behind the house. He had a cloth sack of sunflower seeds. He was drunk. He pushed the seeds into the dirt with his fore-finger. The sky looked like the roof of the diorama. This was Patagonia. He was part of the exhibit. He did not con-sistently believe that. He did not believe it now. But he will believe it again.

At the instance of his mother, a red-beezered monsignor was soon found in the wings, ready to counsel him. The monsignor told Payne that if he kept "it" up he would roast like a mutton over eternal fire. Whatever it was that Payne answered, it made the monsignor leap with agita-tion. It nearly came to blows.

Payne ascended the stairs of the bank building to the county treasurer's office. He was looking for a job. The stairs circled above the green skylight of the bank on the first floor. Somehow the whole beastly building started to bulge, started to throb. And he dropped his briefcase through the skylight. A file clerk looked up at him through the hole. And Payne saw that it was better to be looked up at through the hole, crazy as you were, than to be the file clerk looking.

He began thinking in terms of big time life changes, of art and motorcycles, mountains, dreams and rivers.

Stay for the sunrise. This dude is the color of strawberry. It creeps up Bangtail Creek and flowers through spruce. It stripes the ceiling of the wagon, tints the porous Hudson, and makes, through the screen, something *wild* of Payne's face.

9

Unbeknownst to Payne, a rare blackfooted ferret, which to a colony of gophers is somewhere between C. C. Rider and Stagger Lee, darted from its lair and crossed County Road 67 between Rainy Butte and Buffalo Springs, North Dakota; not far, actually, from the Cedar, which is the south fork of the Cannonball River. This rare tiny savage crittur came very close to being (accidentally) run over by C(letus) J(ames) Clovis, the round-man of total bat tower dreams, who pressed Westward in his Dodge Motor Home.

In a single swoop, Clovis had justified at least a summer's expenditure. Using only local labor and acting himself as strawboss, he raised his bat tower in the West and provided the first bugfree conditions for the American Legion picnic in Farrow, North Dakota. He had watched with a certain joy the bats ditch their high native buttes and come clouding in along the dry washes and gravel bars, through willows and cottonwood, bats in trees and sky pouring like smoke from their caves and holes, bluffs and hollow mesa dwellings, toward the first Western Clovis Batwork with its A-1 accommodations. At the little "Mayan" entrances, there were bat battles. It was—and had to be—first come first served. For a short time, the rats in the bats prevailed; on the little tiered loggias, fearful bat war broke out. And underneath, a worried C. J. Clovis stood with his first client, Dalton Trude, mayor of Farrow, and listened to the distant scuffle. Presently, victims of the fray began to fall; black Victorian gloves; deathflap.

But once things settled down and the various freak bats of anarchy were either knocked off or sent back to the bluffs, Clovis could see that the tower would work. Two days later, the picnic was held and at dusk the bats gathered high over the hot dogs, fried chicken and a whole shithouseload of potato salad. Quite on its own, a cheer went up. Hurrah! Hurrah for them bats! Hurrah for American Legion Farrow Chapter Picnic! Hurrah for C. J. Clovis of Savonarola Batworks Inc. Hurrah!

Clovis set out.

He nearly hit a blackfooted ferret. He crossed the Cedar or south fork of the Cannonball River between Rainy Butte and Buffalo Springs, North Dakota.

C. J. Clovis headed for Montana.

A lowering sky carried smoke from the pulp mill through Livingston. Payne looked at rodeo pictures on the wall of the Longbranch Saloon, refused another drink with a righteous flourish. During the night the northwesternmost block of Main Street burned to the ground. The twenty-four residents of the Grand Hotel escaped without harm. A fireman ran in confusion out of a dress shop carrying a flaming dummy, crying, "You'll be all right!" The dummy was not all right. It turned into a pool of burning plastic and gave off noxious black smoke for hours. A pair of chaps belonging to a man who had been on the burial detail at the Battle of the Little Big Horn were lost without trace. So was a Mexican saddletree with a silver pommel. So was a faggot's collection of bombazine get-ups. So was a bird, a trap, a bolo. All that truck, without a trace.

Payne walked around the fire zone. Adamant volunteers capered around the hook-and-ladder, dousing ashes and trying things out. The hotel appeared to be quite all right; but the lack of windows, the unusual darkness of the interior said no one was home. Possibly only a Commie.

Glass was scattered clear across Main. The plate window of Paul's Appliance Mart blew when the walls buckled and the second story fell into the cellar. The prescription file of City Drug was salvaged and moved to Public Drug where orders will be filled as per usual. A precautionary soaking of the Western Auto roof produced unusual water damage. Bozeman sent their biggest pumper and four firemen. Let's hear it for Bozeman. "Livingston teens were helpful in 'cleaning out' City Drug," the mayor said ambiguously. The *Livingston Enterprise* mentioned "raging inferno," "firemen silhouetted against the flames," a "sad day for all concerned" and various persons "bending over backwards."

That, thought Payne, gazing at the wrack and ruin, is the burned-down block of my hopes, doused by the hook and ladders of real life. Some varmint signed me up for a bum trip. And, quite honestly, I don't see why.

It looked like rain. Nevertheless, art had raised its head. Ann brought her books inside, field guides and novels; and stood the field glasses on the hall table. She took her camera out of its case and mounted it on the aluminum tripod before pulling on her slicker and going outside again. She folded the tripod and carried the whole thing over her shoulder like a shovel. and crossed the yard, climbed through the bottom two strands of wire and dodged manure all the way to the unirrigated high ground where the sage grew in fragrant stripes of blue. The lightning was shivering the sky and it scared her enough that she prudently avoided silhouetting herself on hill tops. When she finally set the camera up, she had no even ground and had to prop the tripod with stones. She checked frequently through the view finder until she felt she had it plumb and began composing. The view finder isolated a clear rectangle of country; three slightly overlapping and declining hills, quite distant; evening light spearing out from under dense cloud cover. The hills divided the frame in a single vibrant line; and though she thought there was something tiresome and Turneresque about the light spears, she liked the incandescence of the cottonwoods whose shapes gently spotted the sharp contours of hill. She had trained herself to previsualize all color into a gray scale so that she could control the photograph in black and white. It pleased her to see the scale here would be absolute. The white, searing lightning with its long penumbra of flash, graded across the viewed area to the pure black shadows in the draws and gullies. Ann felt this polarity of light with an almost physical apprehension; the lightning thrusts seemed palpable and hard. She turned the lens slightly out of focus to exaggerate the contours of the composition; then returned it to a razor edge. She held her breath as though shooting a rifle and kept her hand cradled under the lens, looking down at its pastel depth-of-field figures, the three aluminum legs opening from under the camera like a star. A light perspiration broke out upon her upper lip as she pared away, focusing, selecting aperture and shutter speed toward the pure photographic acuity she perceived in her imagination. The lightning would have to be in it or the picture would be a silly postcard. But it was flashing irregularly and she never knew when it would appear. She wanted it distant and to the left of the lower end of the hills for decent compositional equipoise. As the storm, still distant, increased, the bolts of lightning appeared with greater regularity, a regularity Ann began to feel was rhythmical. She attempted to anticipate this rhythm so that she could trip the shutter at the suitable moment; at each plunge of lightning, at each searing streak, she tightened her muscles and gradually closed in on the interval until, after a dozen or more instances, she stood away from the camera with the cable release in her fingers and moved—very slightly—from head to toe. Her eyes were closed, it must be said. After some moments of this strenuous business, she opened her eyes, dazed, and tripped the shutter at the microsecond that the lightning shimmered, distant, over the lower end of hills. Black and white, diminishing grays were, she knew, stilled and beautiful across thirty-five millimeters of silver nitrate emulsion inside her little camera.

Ann panted there for some time before gathering the legs of the tripod and heading back down toward the ranch.

She felt at one with things.

She felt as if, plumb tuckered, she had blown her wad. She knew that inside her box was an undeveloped image awaiting the bath of real chemicals. Her mind and heart rang with these volleys of zickers. Her step was springy. And her desirable little ass was tight and peach-cleft with girlish go. Aristotle says Eudemonia, she thought.

LAUREL, MONTANA
FRIENDLY CHURCHES
COME
SEE
US

It won't be long now, thought Clovis. Billings was behind at last. To the immediate right of the controls was the television. Clovis had turned it on and was watching The, Dating Game. An attractive adolescent girl had just won two weeks in Reno with a glandular Chief Petty Officer. She had picked him because his voice reminded her of Neil Sedaka. But when he came out from behind the curtain, the girl was agog.

The summer mountains were the color of cougars. In the foreground, a flippant Burma-Shave antagonism manifested itself. Horses stood in the shade of larger signs and switched. Clovis was thinking of Payne's youthful power. It won't be long now, he reminded himself.

Is this fair, Payne asked himself, is it? He looked out of the window of the Big Horn cafe. There was a crowd in the street watching the wreckage of the fire: cowboys, loggers, businessmen, a camel. A young schoolteacher was having lunch with a promising student. "Once you get the drop on Shakespeare," the teacher said, "you've got the whole deal licked." The mayor arrived outside.

A wrecking ball came through a half-burned building, an old mortician's shop, raining pieces of unfinished headstone, tongue and groove siding, bird and mouse nests. A small group had formed around the mayor who gestured toward the fire damage with one upraised palm. "We're gonna prettify this son of a bitch or die trying," he assured his constituency.

"I don't like my work," Payne told an elderly waitress. "Never mind that," she said. "Have a bromo, honey." "I'm unhappy with my lot," he told her.

Ann wasn't small. She was delicately made though and long rather than particularly slender though she was slender too; but what impressed you about her hands, nose and feet was their length and the paleness of her skin. Her eyes seemed very fully open, the upper lid nearly invisible and the lower seeming pared away to a sliver, though without the usual quality of staring. When she smoked, she handled a cigarette with careless precision and could leave a cigarette in her mouth, breathing and squinting through the smoke, and look rather beautiful doing it. She listened attentively even to Wayne Codd who had decided that, after the honeymoon in Paris, they would just constantly be going to operas.

On that appointed day, Payne watched Main Street from the crack of dawn. And at the crack of dusk, the great Dodge appeared, blocking the end of North Main and browsing up the center line with the head of the immortal fatty craning around the inside.

Payne jumped up from his seat in front of the Peterson Dewing building and ran alongside the vehicle. They shook hands through its window and Payne rode on its step while Clovis hunted a forty-foot parking spot.

They camped that night on Bangtail Creek, leaving the Dodge behemoth on the highway. They schemed like Arabs until the morning and rose at first light. Payne built a fire in a small wheelbarrow he found; and in the morning chill, they moved the wheelbarrow around to keep in the sun. They warmed their hands and planned it all.

There was time to go over it later; but, perhaps, Payne

began to see as he had not seen before that in certain important ways his own life, like Clovis', was not funny; or only limitedly so, like cakewalking into a barrage; or better, one of Clovis' horrific signs, the Uncle Sam, for instance, shriveled, asking for a pick-me-up. Payne's indirection took him strangely, as though he were coming down with it, feckless flu. The headlong approach of C. J. Clovis made him, in his vigor and arrogance, the stick in the candy apple of America; it filled Payne with the joy of knowing that expressways are inhabited by artful dodgers, highhanded intuitive anarchists who don't get counted but believe in their vast collective heart that the U.S.A. is a floating crap game of strangling spiritual credit. Write that down.

Clovis saw quite another thing in Payne.

10

C. J. Clovis stood on a bench in Sacajawea Park at Livingston, Montana, haranguing an audience composed of cranks and drifters not unlike himself, on the subject of bat towers. Bats in Clovis' description were tiny angels bent on the common weal, who flittered decoratively through the evening sky ridding the atmosphere of the mosquito. Now the mosquito to Clovis was a simple pus-filled syringe with wings. Was that what you wanted your air filled with? If so, never mind bat towers. If not, contact Savonarola Batworks, Incorporated, poste restante, Livingston, Montana.

"Dear Governor Wallace," wrote Ann to the famous Alabaman. "As an American artist, I would like to offer my condolences for your deceased wife. Rest assured that your darling Lurleen awaits you in Hillbilly Heaven. Sincerely yours, Ann Fitzgerald." Ann was constantly ready to lace into rednecks and right-wingers.

The clear shadow advanced across the parquet floor of her bedroom. She had been in the room since dawn making marks on the floor, every hour on the hour, numbering the shadow's progress to indicate the time. An imperfect plan, she thought, but I'll always be able to glance at it in August and know *quelle heure est-il*. I never come except in August. She sings "Stars Fell on Alabama" in a quiet, pretty voice. Her attitude toward Governor Wallace begins to soften.

Her thoughts of Payne are sporadic and persistent; there has been a pattern. Thoughts of love upon waking in the morning. Thoughts of deprivation then fulfillment on the great unwobbling pivot just before lunch. In the late afternoon, she often thinks of him with anger. Why does he act like that? In the light of the present household tensions, which are terrifically nonspecific, Montana itself begins to pall and subsequently the West, America and so on. As the features of the world recede, Payne is left high and dry like a shipwreck in a drained reservoir. Ann longs to move longingly among his waterlogged timbers, carrying the key to his sea chest. Angelfish, Beau Gregories, tautogs, lantern fish, sergeant majors, morays, bullheads, barracudas, groupers, tunas, flounders, skates, rays, sea robins, balao and narwhals gasp on waterless decks as Ann runs through Payne's bulkheads.

Payne walked across the town to the railroad station where he had left the car. The wagon remained at Bangtail Creek; he hoped not very seriously that it hadn't been vandalized. Underneath the trees on the long lawn beside the station, Pullman porters took the air, chatting with each other and with conductors over the noise of steel-wheeled wagons trucking luggage into the station. Payne wanted to ride the Northern Pacific to Seattle, sitting with Ann in the observation car; perhaps jotting in a pigskin diary: *My Trip*.

I sometimes see myself, thought Payne, in other terms

than standing on the parapets with my cape flying; but not all that often.

Payne did not carry a pistol and tried not to limp.

Payne watched Clovis eat. Clovis was a nibbler; not the kind that doesn't like to eat but the kind who tantalizes himself and makes the food last. Between nips, Clovis described the deal he'd made to build a bat installation in the top stage of an abandoned granary. Payne was to do the building by way of preparing himself for larger projects. It was to be called either a "Bathaus," a "Batrium" or a "Battery"; but, in no case, a "Bat Tower"; the latter being reserved for the all-out projects of Clovis' dreams.

The bat installation was being constructed for a prosperous rancher/wheat farmer whose wife liked to shell peas outside in the evening. She was allergic to 6-12 and Off.

"What if these towers draw vampires?" Payne inquired without getting an answer. Clovis nipped and nibbled, occasionally touching the merest tip of his tongue to a morsel and re-examining it before popping the whole item down his gullet.

Payne watched him. He was draped over his bones. The appliance was the only thing that seemed alive. A morbid air radiated from the man, a certain total mortality that made Payne think rather desperately of Ann.

"What are you gulping for?" Payne asked Clovis, who was swallowing air.

"I am filling my air sac."

"Why?"

"Oh, because despair is my constant companion, I guess."

Payne thought: *what?*

"I didn't see any mention of it in the Yellow Pages."

"What's in them Yellow Pages is between me and the phone company," said Clovis.

"Okay."

"So don't throw the Yellow Pages in my face."

"And those loony signs you had signed your name to in that alleyway off Gratiot Avenue."

"Yeah, what's wrong with them?"

"They're unpatriotic!"

In a single violent motion, Clovis pulled the little pistol from the back of his waist band. Payne snatched it away and shot holes in the tires of the Hudson Hornet. "You want to hurt me?" he said. "There! Now my Hornet won't go any place!" His voice broke.

"I didn't mean a thing . . ." Clovis was upset now.

"You didn't? You pulled that pistol!" Payne's throat ached and seized. He thought he was going crazy. Bangtail Creek beside them roared like an airplane. Mayflies and caddises hatched from its surface and floated toward the stars. Two hundred yards above, it formed its first pool where a coyote made rings in the water around his nose.

The noise of the creek had prevented this small member of the dog family from hearing the argument.

Later, they went over to the Dodge Motor Home and watched Johnny Carson. Ed McMahon infuriated Clovis and he yelled at the television. The guests were Kate Smith, Dale Evans, Oscar Levant, Zsa Zsa Gabor and Norman Mailer, the artist. Johnny smiled with his eyes but not his mouth; and did all these great deadpan things. The big thing was that his outfit really suited him to a "T." Then they watched the Late Show: *Diamondhead;* beautiful Hawaii, very complicated, very paradoxical. They actually had cowboys. But what held your interest was this unique racial deal which was dramatized by Yvette Mi-

mieux falling in love with a native who was darkskinned. It occurred to Clovis that since the Johnny Carson show was taped, it was possible Johnny and his guests were home watching the Late Show too.

"Is there no longer any decency?" Clovis asked.

Payne went back to his wagon to sleep. He could see, hanging in the unnatural pallor of moonlight, a heavy flitch of bacon. Vague boxes of breakfast cereal, dull except where their foil liners glittered, stood next to uneven rows of canned goods. Frying pans hung by pots hung by griddles; and in the middle of all these supplies, next to a solid sewn sack of buckwheat, a radiant Coleman lantern with a new silk mantle began to burn down for the night.

When they awoke, Payne made breakfast for the two of them over his camp stove. The deep balsamic odor of the back country surrounded them. Payne noticed the unseemly slouch the Hornet had on its slumped tires and viewed his own pathology with a certain historical detachment.

"These Little Brown Bats are starting to give me a pain in the ass," Clovis said.

"What are you going to do about it?"

"Probably nothing. I had an idea I could make a go with this Yuma Myotis; but its natural range is too frigging southerly I believe. I have seen the bastards in mine shafts as far west as Idaho; but I don't know." He was quiet briefly. "I'm not starting on an exotic God damn bat breed at this point in my life!"

Payne tried for an intelligent remark. "The thing is, you want something that can really scarf bugs."

"Oh, hell, they all do that. I could take a Western Pipestrel and have the little son of a bitch eating his weight in June bugs night after night. This here is a question of

96

style, a question of class. I want a classy bat! And I don't want something that has to be near running water or has to live in a narrow slot or within two miles of eucalyptus or that sucks the wind for rabies. What's the difference. The Little Brown is okay. That goes for the Silverhaired. But no one is going to pretend they're class bats by a long shot."

"What's . . . a class bat, for instance?"

"Well, no Myotis! That's for damn sure!"

"What then?"

"Almost anything, Payne, for God sake. Leafnose, there's a nice bat. Western Mastiff: that sonofabitch will curl your hair to look at him close. The Eastern Yellow is a good one. The Pallid, the Evening, the Mexican Freetail, the Spotted, the Western Yellow." When he paused, Payne handed him his breakfast on a paper plate. When his voice came again it was mellifluous and sentimental.

"I once owned me a Seminole bat. He was mahogany brown and he looked like he had the lightest coating of frost over him. He weighed a third of an ounce at maturity and was a natural loner."

"Did you name him?"

"Yes I did. I named him Dave."

"I see."

The red Texaco star was not so high against the sky as the Crazy Mountains behind it. What you wanted to be high behind the red Texaco star, thought its owner, was not the Crazy Mountains, or any others, but buildings full of people who owned automobiles that needed fuel and service. Day after day, the small traffic heading for White Sulphur Springs passed the place, already gassed up for the journey. He got only stragglers; and day after day, the same Cokes, Nehis, Hires, Fanta Oranges, Nesbitts and

97

Dr. Peppers stood in the same uninterrupted order in the plastic window of the dispenser. Unless he bought one. Then something else stared out at him, the same; like the candy wrappers in the display case with the sunbleached wrappers; or the missing tools on the peg-board in the garage whose silhouettes described their absence.

That is why Payne coming at the crack of dawn, rolling a herd of flat tires, pursuing the stragglers all over the highway, seemed unusual enough that the station owner helplessly moved a few imperceptible steps toward him in greeting. "Nice day."

"Yes it is."

"Right in here with them uns. Blowouts is they?"

"Yes."

"I see that now. I hope they can be saved."

"They'll have to be."

The man worked furiously taking the tire off the rim of the first. "That's one puncture!" There was a rattle; he fished around. "This tire has been shot!"

"Yes, sir."

The man looked up bemused and went to the next tire. "What kind of recaps is these?"

"Six-ply Firestone Town and Country. Self-cleaning tread."

"This here's been shot too."

"Yup."

The man stood, turning his sweating forehead into the corner of his elbow. "I ain't going no further."

"What do you mean?"

"What do I *mean?*"

"What do you mean?"

"I mean that there has been a shooting here."

"I just want my damn tires fixed."

"Just fix em, heh, no querstions asked? Like ole Docior

Mudd fixing Booth's leg? Let me ask you this. Have you ever read yer history? Let me ask you that."

"No."

"Let me give you a little background then."

"I don't want any background. I want these tires fixed."

"I don't move without an explanation."

The two men were desperate. Payne had nowhere else to turn. The station owner was dealing with his first customer in some time. Payne initiated the detente.

"I shot them myself," he said.

"That's all I needed to hear." The man wiped his hands on a brick-colored rag. "In fact that's just plain more like it." He commenced putting a hot-patch on the first tire. "Honesty is the best policy," he added.

"Oh fuck you," Payne inserted.

"You can say that if you want now. I got no quarrel with you. But when you come in here and want me to start fixing what is plainly the results of a shooting why, you're starting to eat in on my professional ethics."

"I'm going to start screaming."

"I am not going to a federal penitentiary in order to protect a dollar and a half's worth of repair biness."

"I'm going to yell fire."

"What do these go to?"

"They go to a Hudson Hornet."

The man finished and charged Payne three dollars. Payne told him he thought he had been protecting a dollar and a half's worth of biness. "Rate went up," said the man, "with complications of a legal nature."

"That Hornet," he said, "was quite an automobile. Step down in if memory serves. Had quite an engine. Put your foot in the carb and she'd go apeshit to get off the line."

"Yeah only mine doesn't go apeshit no matter where you put your foot."

"She get you over the road?"

"Barely."

"That's all you want," said the owner, racking his mind for a pun about going over the road barely.

"One day," Payne said, fantasizing aggressively, "I'm going to have me a Ford Stepside pickup with the 390 engine and a four-speed box. I want a stereo tapedeck too with Tammy Wynette and Roy Acuff and Merle Haggard cartridges."

"Sure, but that engine. You crash the dude and it's all she wrote." The owner though had picked up on Payne's fantasy. He wanted the same truck, the same stereo cartridges.

"I want to put the cocksucker on 90. I want to go to British Columbia. I want music on the way."

"You do have something there."

The station owner helped Payne take the tires out of the garage. Payne gave them a roll and the tires raced each other down the incline, peeled away and fell in overlapping parabolas to stop near the pumps. Payne rounded them up and got them all going at once, running and yipping around them like a lunatic. When one tried to streak away, he booted it back in line sternly.

By the time he had ridden herd all the way back to the camp, he had named the four tires: Ethel, Jackie, Lady Bird—and Ann.

It was good to have such spirits today. He had bluffs to call.

11

Somewhat experimentally, Ann let her hair hang out of the second story window. Black and rather ineffective against the logs, her beautiful, oval, foxlike face nonetheless glowed against the glassy space behind her.

She retreated inside and began to clean up her room. Protractors, lenses, field guides, United States Geodetic Survey topographical maps, cores of half-eaten apples, every photograph of Dorothea Lange's ever reproduced, tennis shorts, panties, a killing jar, a mounting board, fatuous novels, a book about theosophy, a bust of Ouspensky, a wad of cheap Piranesi prints, her diplomas and brassieres, her antique mousetraps, her dexamyl and librium tablets, her G-string, firecrackers, bocci balls and flagons, her Finnish wooden toothbrush, her Vitabath, her target pistol, parasol, moccasins, Pucci scarves, headstone rubbings, buffalo horns, elastic bandages, mushroom keys, sanitary napkins, monogram die for stationery, Elmer Fudd mask, exploding cigars, Skira art books, the stuffed burrowing owl, the stuffed, rough-legged hawk, the stuffed tanager, the stuffed penguin, the stuffed chicken, the plastic pomegranate, the plaster rattlesnake ashtray, the pictures of Payne sailing, shooting, drinking, laughing, reading comics, the pictures of George smiling gently in a barrera seat at the Valencia Plaza de Toros, an annotated *Story of O*, the series of telephoto shots of her mother and father duking it out beside the old barge canal in Washington, D. C., Payne's prep school varsity jacket, an English saddle, a lid of Panama Green, Charlie Chaplin's unsuccessful autobiography, dolls, a poster from the movie *Purple Noon*, a menu from the Gallatoire restaurant, one from the Columbia in Tampa, one from Joe's Stone Crab in Miami and one from Joe Muer's in Detroit, and one rolled skin from a reticulated python curled around the base of a stainless steel orbiting lamp from Sweden—in short, a lot of stuff lay wall to wall in a vast mess, upon which she threw herself with energy born of her separation from Nicholas Payne.

Within all of her reflections pertaining to him, some in her fantastic style, some in her rational, there permeated the mood of impossibility. Rationally, she knew her training barred a love affair *in extenso* with a man who could describe himself as a cad, someone who had little enough esteem for the *structure* of her background, anthropologically speaking, to call her father "a jerk-off." But in the back of her mind, a tiny voice told her that Payne was someone whose impossibilities could be adapted to expand her spiritual resources. Nothing happened she couldn't outgrow; but what bothered a little—sometimes—was that Nicholas, through some total romantic frangibility, didn't have quite the same resilience. His emotional losses had a way of turning out to be real ones. It was like in books and made her jealous.

Here, in a funny way, a considerable moral precision was seen in Ann; and it was a faculty that refracted from quite another part of her than that which had her hang her head from the window, hair against logs. And stranger still, it was this part, not the Rapunzel, which made her once so limp with love for Payne, the cad, Pecos Bill; that put her under such a spell that to see him at all would be to cut her moorings forever on a risk no one was recommending.

She read somewhere that love was an exaggeration that only led to others; and she seized on the notion. She wanted a subtler scale of emotions than it offered. She was exhausted by the bruising alternation from ecstasy to despair. For someone who believed she might have been an honest-to-God intellectual, it was humiliating. During that first winter, she and Nicholas would walk on the Lake Erie shore making plenty sure that the desolating wave wrack of human debris didn't touch their feet; involved either in total spiritual merger or agonizing disharmony; remembering it now, she could only think of the lurid, metallic sunsets, the arcs of freighter smoke and the brown tired line of Canada beyond.

And, too, these alternations had a certain cosmic niftiness, a Heathcliff and Cathy finality that gave her a sense of their importance. And the secrecy was good. No one knew they were down in his boat copulating in the rope bunk, night after night. No one knew they launched citizens of their own to the condom-city that had been triangulated between Cleveland, Buffalo and Detroit. No one knew that they had chipped in and sent the Mother Superior at Payne's grade school a tantalizing nightie from Frederick's of Hollywood with the note, "To a real *Mother Superior!*" No one knew, despite Payne's opposition to Lozenge, that she felt transcendentally affixed to every day that passed for an entire winter.

Now, from a handy tree in central Montana, Wayne

Codd watched Ann fall upon her bed in the debris-filled room to weep wretchedly, spasmodically. What a sight! He put the binoculars down from his eyes, having banished a rather piddling inclination to self-abuse. The hell with it. They was work to do. He felt the imperial blue of the West form in his eyes. He felt the virile prominence of the cowboy in the mythographical ecosystem of America. Like a sleek and muscular hyena, he knew the expendability of chumps and those who weep, that the predators, the eagles of humanity, might soar. He shinnied down ready for ranching. *He* hadn't cried since he was a child.

For Missus Fitzgerald, the handwriting on the wall was about to appear as a lurching mechanical hysteria which took—in this incarnation—the form of a Hudson Hornet.

For Payne, driving along and listening to the livestock reports—"These fat steers is dollaring up awful good"—it was not as easy as it looked; a vast fungo-bat of reality seemed to await him in the Shields Valley; to be precise, in the vicinity of the Double Tepee or Squaw Tits Ranch. But it would do to say in his favor that the old fidgeting approach, the old obliquity, was gone. No, frightened as he might be, he would arrive head-on.

Little comfort derived from the slumbrous heat of the day. It was a flyblown hot summer to begin with; but this bluebottle extravaganza of shimmering terrain didn't seem like anything you would call Montana. The animals were running crazy and dead game was all over the highway. The creeks were trickles. Their trout hid in springs and cutbanks. A long mountain bluff ended on the side of the road, the merest tongue tip of a yawning universe.

As he drove, he had a bird's-eye view of his own terror. High, high above the mountain West, Payne saw an automobilicule, microscopic, green, creeping up a hairline valley between wen-size mountains. The driver was too small to be seen. The horizon was curved like a boomerang. Payne "chuckled goodnaturedly" at the tiny driver you couldn't even see who thought his fear saturated everything down to the Pre-Cambrian core. How naughty!

God the Father was out here somewhere; as to the Holy Spirit, he merely whirled quietly in a culvert, unseen by anyone.

Payne turned the radio dial irritably, getting only British rock music. It maddened him. What a smutty little country England had become, exporting all its Cro-Magnon song dodos, its mimsy, velveteen artistes. Payne wanted Richie Valens or Carl Perkins, and now.

Missus Fitzgerald, trying to make up for snippish words and a recent attack involving ballpoint pens, made with her own red hands a rich cassolette of duck and pork and lamb and beans. With her great Parisian balloon whisk she beat a pudding in an enormous tin-lined copper bowl; and set it—trembling—on the drainboard.

Payne lifted the front gate and swung it aside, stepping carefully across the cattle guard. His hands were trembling. He drove the car through, got out and closed the gate behind himself.

Along the road to the ranch buildings, a small fast stream ran, much diminished, and where it made turns were broad washes of gravel from the spring run-off. Scrub willow grew here, and on the cliffbanks were the holes of swallows. Then came the mixed woodland that Payne could not have known was the last stretch of geography between himself and the house. That it was composed of larch, native grass and bull pine held no interest for him. He had to go to the bathroom quite a lot. A relatively small band of pure American space seemed to throw a step-over-toe-hold on his gizzard.

Payne made no attempt to lighten his tread on the porch and, before thought, gave the door a good pounding. Mister and Missus Fitzgerald opened the door together stretching their arms to him, paternally and maternally. In the long warmly lit corridor Ann stood shyly murmuring "darling." They took him inside, warming him with their bodies; everyone, it seemed, tried to hold his hand. "May we call you son?" Ann cried with happiness. They leaped to each other, kissed with youthful passion, held each other at arm's length. "At last!" A beaming, lusty preacher moved forward as though on a trolley, supporting a Bible with one hand and resting the other on top of it.

Payne made no attempt to lighten his tread on the porch and, before thought, gave the door a good pounding. He heard someone move and was afraid. Frequent nerve farts troubled the silence. He thought: Windex, buffalo, Zaragoza. He knocked once more and the door behind the little grate opened at eye level. Nary a sound was heard. He knocked again, stood quietly and knocked once more. A weary voice, that of Mister Fitzgerald, was heard from the grill. "I hear you, I hear you. I'm just trying to think what to do about you."

"Let me in."

The door opened suddenly. "Right you are," said Fitzgerald. "God help us." He shut the door. "Follow me." Fitzgerald pulled him into the hallway. Payne followed him down to a small utility room. "Stay here." Fitzgerald left.

Payne stood very nearly without motion for ten or fifteen minutes. Nothing. The washing machine stopped and a few minutes later the dryer, which also had been running, whirled to a stop. Payne idly opened the washing machine and saw the still wet clothes pressed centrifugally to the walls of its tumbler. The door opened behind him.

Missus Fitzgerald's voice came from behind him. "Who are you?"

Payne turned, stood, smiled. Her face was more delicate than a casserole.

"*GET OUT*"

When sophisticated or wealthy women get angry, they attempt to make their faces look like skulls. Missus Fitzgerald did this and looked awfully like a jack-o-lantern. She was that fat.

Payne offered to explain.

"*GET OUT!*" She just said that. "*HE'S IN OUR HOUSE!*" she added, taking credit for a discovery that was not hers.

"I can—"

"NO!"

"I can—"

"NO!"

"No, what?"

"YOU CAN'T . . . YOU HAVE TO GET OUT!"

Somewhere along in here she began scoring heavily with a plumber's friend with which she belabored Payne. He shielded himself and sought protection behind the hampers. "You've got crime written all over you," she panted. He seized the plumber's friend, suppressed an itch to beat the living piss out of her with it. Fitzgerald arrived, having allowed a leisurely ripening of the scene.

"You jerk," said Fitzgerald, "you didn't know when a

107

favor had been done for you." He chuckled grimly to himself. "Do you realize," he asked, "that when the Second World War was raging and Hitler was riding high that I was the squash champion of the Detroit Athletic Club?" This stopped everything.

"What has that got to do with anything!" his wife, Edna, wailed. Fitzgerald started into a long song and dance about the kind of guy he was. And though there was considerable poignancy in his latest fatuity, its effect was to shatter Missus Fitzgerald's primitive stagecraft of shrieks and accusations.

"Ann!" Payne bellowed after some thought, trying to bring things to life. He caught the right note; because Fitzgerald lunged to shut him up. But Payne could not mistake the sound of her skittering descent of the stairs, one hand on the rail, the which seemed to last an eternity.

As she appeared, he commenced cowering before her parents. They melted under her glare. Payne saw her, his spirit twining and tautening. Before him, the one true. They smiled amid the total inutility of this bug scuffle. Discreetly, Ann recorded everything with her camera, including a final blow with the plunger.

"Neutral corners," cried Fitzgerald.

"Are we not ever to be safe?" inquired his wife. Payne quietly turned the washing machine on again.

"I can explain everything," he said with sudden blind joy.

"We don't want to hear!"

"Maybe you should," Ann said, her voice a saffron buffalo trotting to Jerusalem with a pony express mailbag of loving hellos. "Maybe you ought to."

"Are we not ever to be safe from the depredations of this criminal?"

"Edna," said Fitzgerald in the plainsong of common sense.

"Never?" A minute fissure had appeared in her voice.

"Edna," Payne said.

"I want someone to tell me," she said with a noble, judicial mien—as though her voice was making an independent threat to cry—"I'm prepared to make other arrangements with my own life if we are to be repeatedly and casually displaced by the depredations of this hoodlum . . . Catholic criminal type."

"Oh, now Edna."

"I'm a backslider," said Payne. "There's many an empty day between me and my last novena."

"I have my wig bank, as silly as that may sound. But there is work for me."

"No, no, no. Payne will be gone. You'll see."

A flash of hatred as can only be produced by an inconvenienced businessman arced from Fitzgerald's eyes to those of Payne. Payne wanted so much to have a showdown; but he knew it would come to nothing with Ann. It was part of her style to present herself as an integral part of a noble family package.

On the other hand, when her father took Payne by the throat and attempted to strangle him, it was Ann who tore free his hands.

This was another mistake for Fitzgerald; its unseemliness even drove his wife from the room. She went out saying she no longer saw how it would be possible to inhabit this ranch.

"This hasn't been a satisfactory show," tried Fitzgerald, winningly, "on the part of the Missus and myself."

"Frankly, the part with the toilet plunger left me cold." It had become difficult to be heard over the washing machine. It shuddered and wobbled in a steam-laden surge. Engine-driven, Payne imagined, it whirled a sacred cargo of Ann's little things.

"Daddy," Ann said, "it's too late for this kind of . . . *protection.*"

"It's hard to face that, honey."

"But you must."

"I know that darling. I see that too. We never interfered much before, did we? Before Payne broke into the house? Did we darling? And bombarded Mom with filth when she found him in the library? Did we? But, kids, try and see it my way, huh? Nick here screaming that Mom's head wouldn't draw flies at a raree show—that's not good, is it kids? Or is this a generation deal?"

"Can we leave the laundry room?" Payne enquired.

"Let me just say this," Duke Fitzgerald went on. "Ann, do as you wish. We'll honor whatever you decide. And Mom will back me up. I promise."

"I don't know what I wish!"

"Ann—"

"I don't know, Daddy!" Ann didn't want to pair off. She wanted to play in her room with all the junk for a few more years. Fitzgerald, the ghoul, saw it.

"I mean, look, do you want to get married?"

"No one said that," Ann said. Payne was grievously pained. Fitzgerald raised his palms up, both of them to one side of his face in a gesture of assured noninterference.

"You wanna set up house, I'll get outa the way." Fitzgerald could have had the ball game then and there; but a sudden vision of a house without Ann in it, and of his wife charging in with a fistful of ballpoint pens, made him pull back. He lacked—at that moment anyway—an essential killer's instinct.

But Fitzgerald had shown his right, even in this incomplete thrust, to a room at the top. Now he wanted to round things out. "Nick, there's room here for you. Ann'll tell you when we eat." Even that took some restraint. Fitzgerald wanted to promise Payne that if he turned his back it was going to be angel choirs long before he thought he'd ever see them.

"Fine," Payne said, nodding graciously.

"Okay, kid. We've got a deal."

Fitzgerald went to the door and took its handle. He let his head drop a little without turning to look at them. "G'night, Annie," he said thickly and went out.

When he had gone, Ann said, "He never called me Annie before."

Payne seized her. They grappled lovingly among the hampers. A famous man says that we go through life with "a diminishing portfolio of enthusiasms"; and these, these, these *children,* these these these these *little children* will soon not be able to feel this way about anything again.

12

Wayne Codd eased the bunkhouse door shut behind himself and made his way across the open drive to where Payne was unloading a couple of low, tatty, catch-all suitcases. It was not in the least the kind of luggage Codd associated with top-level arrivals at Gallatin Field in Bozeman. The fourteen-carat buckaroos from Dude City Central Casting that poured out of those Northwest Orient Fan Jet Electras didn't go around with deal luggage of that sorry order. It reassured him.

Then the haircut. You couldn't see the bastard's ears. Codd wanted to go up and flat tell Payne that red white and blue were colors that didn't run. Instead, he took the time to estimate Payne as though he were a chine of beef; and he came up with the dispiriting intelligence that Payne was on the big side. Furthermore, he was throwing gear around the back of the wagon in a way that reminded Codd, by special paranoid telepathy, of himself being abused at some future time. He walked over.

"Nice day," Codd said.

"Yes it is." Payne rolled an Indian blanket and packed it beside the camp stove in the front of the wagon.

"Been sure hot."

"Yes it has."

"You workin here naow?"

"Just visiting." He climbed out of the wagon. "I work with another fellow. I guess I'll be staying here a bit though."

"How long?"

"I don't know."

"About how long?"

"I surely couldn't tell you." Payne introduced himself and they shook hands.

"You're not workin here then, ay?"

"No."

"And you're not figurin on workin."

"Why? Do you work here?"

"That's right, friend."

"You sound like a man with a situation to himself," Payne declared.

"I am," Codd said. "I expect to keep it that way."

"Well, it *is* nice to be able to lay back without anybody cracking the whip when you do."

"Yeah, only I don't do that."

"That's even more wonderful."

"I wasn't callin it wonderful," Codd said.

"Well, that's even more whatever you've been finding yourself calling it."

"Uh huh."

"Look," Payne said, "you were the one that came over and talked to me."

"That's so. I was."

"Are you the foreman here?"

113

"Correct."

"Got anything to do right now?"

"Nothin."

"In that event," Payne said, "why don't you buzz back to the bunkhouse and let me get on with the job."

Fitzgerald leaned out of an upper window.

"Wayne, give Nick a hand there if he needs you."

"Run all those suitcases up to the guest room," Payne said, fishing for a cigar in his shirt pocket. "I'll be playing foreman over here at the foot of this tree."

Codd put a forefinger into Payne's chest, prefatory to making a remark of some kind. Payne spoiled his preparation by slapping his hand halfway around his back, establishing specific personal limits.

He lit his cigar and retired to the shade at the foot of the cottonwood. Codd disappeared into the entrance of the house. Fitzgerald smiled overhead . . . at what?

Payne lifted the wagon tongue off the wagon hitch and put his back into moving the son of a bitch under the trees by the tack room where it would be inconspicuous. He planned to use his considerable handiness in helping everyone at the ranch. Then they would all be happy and like one another. Thinking of Ann, of the ranch, of his happiness and good work under the mountains and sunshine, he sings:

> All around the world
> I've got blisters on my feet,
> Trying to find my baby
> And bring her home to me!
> With a toothpick in my hand
> I'd dig a ten-foot ditch!

And run through the jungle
Fighting lions with a switch!
Because you know I love you baby!
Yes you know I love you baby!
Whoa-oh you know I love you baby!
Well, if I don't love you baby:
GRITS AND GROCERIES!
EGGS AND POULTRIES!
AND MONA LISA WAS A MAN!

Ten hours and fourteen and a half minutes earlier, C. J. Clovis had come out of surgery for the removal of his left arm which had been rendered useless and dangerous by a total closure of circulation and the beginnings of gangrene. Whether or not his doctors had been precipitous in the removal of the limb remained to be argued. In any case, they had consulted with his physicians in Michigan, including the singular young surgeon to whom had fallen the unlikable task that ended with lugging the heavy left leg of Clovis across the operating theater to the stainless bin; where it was discarded like tainted meat—which, presumably, it was. As with the amputated leg, the arm, discarded, had shown the baleful, zigzag incisions as though the work had been done with pinking shears.

It took Payne hours to find him in the empty hospital ward, where he rested on that particular fine summer's day. Payne, worse than useless, permitted tears to stream down his cheeks, until Clovis shouted, "Stop it! I may be a goner! Just stop that!"

"I would have stayed up at Bangtail if I had known you were sick."

"I didn't know I was either. This is one fucking mess."

"The doctor said this is the end of it. He said it'll take

115

some getting used to but this is the last thing that's coming off."

"Don't listen to them, Payne. They've scavenged me as it is. I don't know where they're going to stop!"

"They already have stopped."

"But can't you see! With their tin-can optimism they feel no responsibility to be accurate! They just don't want scenes in their waiting rooms! Everybody's going to be okay! And these buggers probably believe it, is the worst of it. They believe everything is going to be okay right up to the point the patient kicks off, then they switch to their famous doctor's resignation in matters of life and death. When those fuckers start in like preachers about doing all that was humanly possible I want to kick their big soft white asses. I want to yell, 'shove your humanly possible! You're dismantling me! My arm is gone! My leg is gone! Now just give me a God damn schedule and I'll know when you're gonna haul off the rest of it!' Here's the kind of deal that floors you, Payne: Where is my arm at this minute?"

After a while, Payne admitted he just didn't know what to say.

"Almost the worst part," Clovis said, "is that I just got a contract for a Batrium."

Payne remembered the breakwater at home.

"I'll do it. I'll build the . . . batrium."

"You don't know how," Clovis said, his face, unbelievably enough, lighting with ambition and greed.

"I'll figure it out."

"I'm so happy. I may as well say it. I am."

Payne sped away with a sense he hadn't had since his paper route. The feeling of the last few days of no longer needing sleep was exaggerated at once.

So, for the next two days, Payne lay upon his back in the

116

top of that silo, in the infraheat of the pure high exposure enhanced by the warmth of fermentation below him. And he carefully nailed, coigned, wedged, butt-blocked, strong-backed, mitered and chamfered the passages of the Clovis Batrium, the sweat pouring out of him in a fog. Even pinch-face, the farmer, admitted that it was "crackerjack carpentry"; and there was no trouble collecting the payment in full which Payne delivered to a rather pleased multiple amputee in the Livingston clinic.

Ann's voice from the stairwell, sandy and musical at once, "Nicholas! Supper!"

"Sit wherever you like," said Missus Fitzgerald with cloying joy at Payne's arrival. "Wherever." Payne placed himself next to Ann. It was quite dark already; though a candelabrum of beeswax candles burned an octopus of light in the gloom. As everyone else arranged themselves, Fitzgerald at the serving dishes, Payne believed he saw, in the far end window, the face of Codd rise, gape and vanish.

"Montana," Missus Fitzgerald said in a heavy twang for the occasion, "is a fur piece from home."

"Anything here not suit you, Mister Payne?" said Fitzgerald.

"Nothing."

"Do you like to travel?" La Fitzgerald.

"I do very much, thank you."

"And where have you been?"

Payne named the places.

La said she had been to all those and more.

"Mother," said Fitzgerald, "is a travel fiend."

"A travel what?"

"Fiend."

"I began," Missus Fitzgerald agreed, "as a young girl, traveling in Italy. The Italians in those days pinched the prettiest girls—"

"Mussolini cleaned that particular clock," said her husband.

"And I," Missus Fitzgerald said, "had to leave the country."

"I see," said Payne, nervous.

"A mass of tiny bruises."

"I uh see."

"Italy, this was Italy."

Payne had to comment.

"It must have been a long time ago, Missus Fitzgerald," he groped. The indelicacy of the remark was invisible to him, glaring to the others. Now, once again, Missus Fitzgerald hated his crime-ridden little guts.

"Mother, Nicholas didn't mean *that*."

"No," said the Mum, "you wouldn't suppose ordinarily."

Payne began to see it and, wordlessly, felt plumb stupid. He was quite unnerved by the situation. The last time they'd had him in the house . . : oh, well, what was the use. It was on everybody's mind. King Kong takes a nosedive. A proclamation of emperor. Magister lewdy at the papal bullfights. Stalked through the house, a shotgun to the lip, a brandy for each ear. Mortal coils was the color of his vita. It was as simple as that.

Payne looked at Ann, saddened that he was not always a man who was in his own driver's seat. By flashes, she was enraged too that he lacked George's polish. And Payne wondered: Will you care for me when I'm old? Will you fork over for two adults in the mezzanine when we hit the Saturday matinee? Or make me sit in the smoking loggia with my cheap cigar, bicycle clips on my pants legs and a card that reads: *The U.S.A. social security props this pot-*

licker up every morning. It is yer duty as a citizen to treat him like a Dutch uncle. Don't make me get old, Mom. Remember me? The boy that wanted to skyrocket into eternity in a white linen suit that showed his deltoids? Don't permit the years to tire him. But then. Well. Isn't it really time that is the shit that hits everybody's fan? Fess up, isn't it? But Ann, to hold my hand when the others have gone and left me with words of foundationless criticism, after whole epochs, the two of us to face the final ditch spewing exalted thoughts like feathers from a slashed pillowcase. Wouldn't that be a dream the regality of which would shut down the special-order department at Neiman-Marcus?

"There," Payne said with clarity. "I feel so much better." They looked at him. He was suddenly blinded with embarrassment; and his mind slipped away, really slipped away. Past the far edge of the gravy boat, he perceived an Oscar Niemeyer condominium high in the cordillera of the Andes. An elderly Brazilian diplomat stood over a young Indian prostitute, a finger raised, his nose in a manual, saying, *"Do that!"*

At the same time, he saw curious things happening in the American West. For instance, at the foot of the Belt Mountains, a young man who had earlier committed the stirring murder of a visiting Kuwait oil baron, ate from a tin and barked *"mudder"* at his captors.

A tall summer thunderhead hung over the valley of the Shields River, in fact, directly over the Fitzgerald ranch, certain of the walls of whose main house hid the little dinner party from the view of nobody whatsoever.

Nobody whatsoever would have been much interested in Payne's discomfort which was quite carefully cultivated by two of the three people around him.

"No," Payne said, "I couldn't eat another turnip."

"Potatoes?"

"No," Payne said, "(*ditto*) potato."

"What about some asparagus?"

"No," said Payne, "(*ditto*) any more asparagus."

"Payne," said Fitzgerald, "what do you want?

"How do you mean?"

"Out of life?"

"Fun."

"Really," said Missus Fitzgerald.

"So do you."

"But," she said, "I'd have hardly put it that way."

"Nor I." Fitzgerald, naturally.

"I would have," said Ann, trying to show her surprise at their remarks. The word "fun" seemed to accrete images of liberation.

"You would have put it," Payne said in a general address to his elders, "more impressively. But you would have meant fun."

"No," said La, "we would have meant something more impressive than fun too."

"You seem to imagine that by fun I mean some darkish netherworld of hanky-panky. Nothing could be farther from the truth."

Fitzgerald shook his head in a wintry smile. The effect, entirely unsubstantiated, was of wisdom.

"What do *you* mean by fun?" Missus Fitzgerald inquired.

"I mean happiness. Read Samuel Butler."

"I assure you we have."

"Do it again."

"Oh, Payne, now," smiled Fitzgerald, his face a study in major Greek pity. "Payne, Payne, Payne."

Payne felt, thinking of his father's furnace, that he wanted to heat the air to incandescence for six cubic acres around the house. "Cut that shit out now," he told Fitz-gerald.

Ann, sensing the feasibility of Nicholas' blowing his stack, raised the tips of conciliatory fingers over the table's edge as in steady there, steady now big feller, don't kick over your oats there now big feller there now you.

"I wanted," Payne said, "merely to have dinner in an agreeable atmosphere. Is generosity no longer available?"

"Ah Payne, Payne, Payne."

"Give it to me straight. I can take it."

The mother told Payne that they had had enough of him. "We merely asked what you believed in," she said. "We had no idea it would precipitate nastiness."

"*What I believe in?* I believe in happiness, birth control, generosity, fast cars, environmental sanity, Coor's beer, Merle Haggard, upland game birds, expensive optics, hel-mets for prizefighters, canoes, skiffs and sloops, horses that will not allow themselves to be ridden, speeches made under duress; I believe in metal fatigue and the immortal-ity of the bristlecone pine. I believe in the Virgin Mary and others of that ilk. Even her son whom civilization ac-cuses of sleeping at the switch." Missus Fitzgerald was seen to leave the room, Ann to gaze into her lap. "I believe that I am a molecular swerve not to be put off by the zippy diversions of the cheap-minded. I believe in the ultimate rule of men who are sleeping. I believe in the cargo of torpor which is the historically registered bequest of poli-tics. I believe in Kate Smith and Hammond Home Organs. I believe in ramps and drop-offs." Fitzgerald got out too, leaving only Payne and Ann; she, in the banishing of her agony and feeling she was possibly close to Something, raised adoring eyes to the madman. "I believe in spare tires and emergency repairs. I believe in the final possum. I believe in little eggs of light falling from outer space and the bombardment of the poles by free electrons. I believe in tintypes, rotogravures and parked cars, all in their places. I believe in roast spring lamb with boiled potatoes. I believe in spinach with bacon and onion. I believe in canyons lost under the feet of waterskiers. I believe that we are necessary and will rise again. I believe in words on paper, pictures on rock, intergalactic hellos. I believe in fraud. I believe that in pretending to be something you aren't you have your only crack at release from the bondage of time. I believe in my own dead more than I do in yours. What's more, *credo in unum deum,* I believe in one God. He's up there. He's mine. And he's smart as a whip.

"Anyway," he said mellifluously and with a shabbily urbane gesture, "you get the drift. I hate to flop the old philosophy on the table like so much pig's guts. And I left out a lot. But, well, there she is."

And it was too. Now and again, you have to check the bread in the oven.

An instant later, he imagined he was singing the Volga boat song. Ann clapped a hand over his mouth. It wasn't the Volga boat song. It was some febrile, mattoid, baying nonsense. No one saw why he should be acting up like this.

"What are you *doing?*" It reminded her of the way people went crazy on TV as opposed to Dostoyevsky.

"Dunno."

He had strained himself.

His feeling was that it was the dining room, the act of eating itself, that dramatized what the Mum, the Dad, had in mind for him. That was what was behind their fierceness over their food; they were pretending it was him, he decided; and he didn't like it from an almost metaphysical plane of objection; to the effect that martyrdom should be represented more strikingly than in platters of meat and vegetables. These things, thought Payne, are not relics. Bits of the true sirloin. He imagined monstrances filled with yams and okra; our beloved smörgåsbord has gone on before.

Payne calmed down. He considered the solemn flummery of the Fitzgeralds' departure, the effect that time was not to be wasted on him. He looked at Ann, becomingly leaning on the table with both elbows. A certain hirsute mollusc came to mind.

"Dinner seemed to fall short of one of those civilized encounters of mind we hear about."

"Yes," Ann said, ungratefully adding, "your fault as much as theirs. It just seems completely uncultivated."

"I think so."

"That kind of silliness could be endless. You'll never tire each other out."

"My silliness means more."

"Oh, I don't know."

"I've made it a way of life," Payne said. "That means something."

"But what are we going to do. I'm so tired of this, this—"

"Yes, me too."

"This, this—"

"Yes," Payne said.

"We could run off," she said, thinking that she could take pictures, making the act of running away itself the unifying factor or theme.

"I see it in my mind's eye," Payne said wearily.

"I mean it though, Nicholas."

"The hobo shot. The American road. We sit in ditches covered with sage and pollen. Cannonades of giant mid-American laughter flood the sky around us; it is ours. We are giants in the earth snagging Strategic Air Command bombers in our hair because it is big hair. That goes up. Where bombers are."

There was a disturbance at the door, a small aggressive shuffling, the lout's movement of Codd.

"I was wondering."

"Yes?" Payne said, the dim view showing.

"If there was anything I could do."

"No, Wayne," Ann said pleasantly. "Thanks, not now."

"But Mister Fitzgerald said to come over and see what I could do."

"Nothing, thanks, Codd," Payne said.

"I was sure that—"

"The old dodo gave you a bum steer," Payne said simply.

"I'll tell him," said Codd with the smile there.

"You tell him that you were given a bum steer by him and had received it in good condition."

"Yes, because he said for me to come see what I could do. But I'll tell him from you that the thing was he had given me this bum steer."

"One other thing, Codd."

"No, you one other thing a minute. I'm thinking of busting you in the God damn mouth."

"No, Codd."

"No, what."

"You won't do that. You'll announce it over and over but in the end you won't do it."

"That's your idea, huh."

"Sure is."

"Well if you get it," Codd said, "don't come cryin to me. Because it'll just be a case of you achin for it and me givin it to you."

"As a guest here I resent the abuse of footlings. Presently, I may be heard to shriek for the management."

"Do it."

"*Peep.* See? My heart's not in it. Codd, one false move and I'll pull your upper lip over the back of your head. And another thing: I love you."

"Then you're a fruit."

"But Ann too, see? It's one of those world brotherhood deals that's liable to end in liquidation. Damn it, I'm washing my hands of you. I'd hoped you'd turn out to be something better than this. Your mother and I had dreamed you'd be the first mate on a torpedoed Nazi destroyer. And I don't know where this leaves us; with our dreams I guess; of what you might have been; if it hadn't been for the war years."

"What you ought to do," Codd said, seeming to know what he was talking about, "is go up to Warm Springs and get yourself certified. Far as I'm concerned, yer too crazy to beat up."

"Yes," said Ann. Her soundest social notion was that everyone in the world was too crazy to beat up.

Codd walked down the hallway, the bulldogging heels of his tiny cowboy boots ringing on the hardwood. With a light feinting gesture of the head, he avoided injury by elk's antler at the corner of the living room; with a low scuttling jump, he avoided entanglement with bearskin at the front of the grotesque travertine fireplace with its iron firedogs and prestolite scented simulogs. Pivoting in a sharp dido around the far entrance to the living room, he was in an identical hallway where, once more, there was the ringing of the tiny boots as his forward bolting posture soon hurtled him through the far screen door. On the lawn, he walked over the cesspool, invisible to him under the sod; among the heavy willows he strode toward his bunkhouse beneath the singular tattoo of Orion.

125

Hanging, later, upended over the dormer window of Ann's room, he watched her mock burlesque before Payne, their subsequent entanglement, her compact uplift of blushing buttock, his paler flesh and hers flaring in their seizure, the long terrific prelude and final, spasmic, conjunctive entry, marked, unknown to either of them, by the gloomy jetting of Codd against the shingles overhead.

Codd, spent, saw the rooftree sink suddenly in his vision, Orion start up, and realized he was falling. In a terror of being perceived hanging from the lintel, his livery about his knees, he launched himself into space, plunged into a lucky willow and merged himself against the heavy rigid trunk while Payne knuckled up and down the sill saying I know you're out there.

Satisfied that it had only been a limb falling, Payne returned to Ann, lying upon her stomach. The peerless, long back arced up at her bottom; Payne sat next to her and slid his hand underneath, thinking this is where Darwin got the notion of primordial ooze; put a speck of it under a microscope and see Shakespeare leaping through time; also, lobsters, salamanders, one coelacanth. He knelt between her thighs, raised her hips, thrust and flooded helplessly. My God. How many fan letters could you seal with that. Enough to get the message across, perhaps. Mock turtle soup.

Leaving Ann's room and proceeding to his own, he passed, in the lugubrious great hall of the house, Mister Fitzgerald, smoking peevishly and adjusting with one glowing foot an ornate iron firedog.

"Evening, sir."

"Well, Payne, good evening."

"Do you want to speak to me?" Payne asked.

"Not at all."

Payne continued past the stone entry of that really funny room and into the glossy varnished passageway to his own quarters. About halfway down that corridor, he ran into Wayne Codd who, from his position within an insignificant shadow cast by a large plaster-of-paris penguin, inquired whether or not Payne would care to fight.

"No," Payne said, and went to his room where he admired the drum-tight Hudson's Bay blanket with its four black lines for the indication of class or general snazz. He had locked the door; but it was a short time before the clicking of Codd's skeleton key groping for the indifferent tumblers of Payne's lock was heard. Payne patted the cool surface of the sheet. "This is a happy Western lodge," he said to himself. "I smell elk in this pillow." Then close to the door, he said, "Wait a minute, wait a minute, I'll unlock it." For a long moment, he made no movement. "You'll have to pull the key out."

"Okay." The key was extracted.

"Come in," Payne said. The knob wrenched and the door did not open.

"It's still locked," came the ululating voice, urgent with wrath.

"Hang on. Just a sec." Payne brushed his teeth. "What did you call me?" No answer, but once more the swift perfect failure of the skeleton key. Payne's ablutions were most complete. He brushed first smartly the teeth then smoothly the hair. He never once poured smoothly the buckwheat batter. He adjusted trimly the clavicles and elevated the coccyx at a racy angle like a Masai. By way of preparation, he bounded around the room in what came to seem a perfect frenzy. Abruptly, he flung open the door, knocked Codd unconscious, closed the door and turned in for the night.

Presently, however, a brisk knocking was heard upon

the door and Payne answered, expecting to find the drear, abnormally expanded face of the recently comatose Codd. Unexpectedly, he found instead Fitzgerald, at pains not to tread upon his foreman.

"What's with him?"

"Receipt of blow to his chops. The hydraulic effect of that, you might say, toward a reduction of consciousness." Fitzgerald stepped over him and entered the room. "I know why you've come."

"You do?"

"*Oui, mon enfant,*" said Payne, "you want to invite me into your family."

"Do you realize how inexpensively I could have you shot?"

"Yes."

"You do?"

"But I'm alarmed you would maintain such connections."

"Well, goodnight then, Payne."

"Goodnight to you sir. I trust these morbid preoccupations of yours will not trouble your sleep. Look at it this way, I could have you shot as cheaply. I presume the price is within both our means."

"Yes, I suppose. Well, goodnight then, Payne." He went out, taking elaborate pains not to step into the face of his foreman, Wayne Codd. Payne went to sleep, moved by the pismire futilities of moguls—their perpetual dreams, that is, of what could be done with the money.

13

A long gliding sleep for Payne was followed by a call to breakfast. He stumbled into the hallway and found himself in some sort of procession, the whole family moving in one direction, deploying finally in silence around a glass pantry table. They were served by an old Indian lady who maintained a stern air that kept everyone silent. Plates were put on the table with unnecessary noise. Then, when it seemed finally comfortable to eat, there was an uproar in the hallway. Behind Codd, darkling with rage, came the fabulous multiple amputee of untoward bat-tower dreams—none the worse for wear—C. J. Clovis, variously sustained with handsomely machined aluminum mechanisms and superstructures; around which the expensive flannel he affected (and now a snap-brim pearly Dobbs) seemed to drape with a wondrous futuristic elegance. The Indian woman stepped through the smoked-glass French doors in petulant response to the noise. Breakfast was ordered for Clovis. The Fitzgeralds arose, smiling gaily aghast. Admittedly, the rather metallurgical surface Clovis presented to the world would have been intimidating to anyone who hadn't been in on the process.

Payne made the introductions. Codd, sporting welts, bowed out. Payne watched him until his attention returned to the others; he found Clovis already selling a bat tower.

"We don't want a bat tower, Mister Clovis," said La.

"In what sense do you mean that?"

"In any sense whatever."

Clovis gave them the encephalitis routine—mosquitoes as pus-filled syringes, et cetera, et cetera—including a fascinating rendition of death by microbe during which his plump sagging little carcass writhed mournfully beneath the abrupt motions of the metal limbs. From the viewpoint of the Fitzgeralds, it was really appalling. Coffee and toast cooled without interference. Fitzgerald himself was perfectly bug-eyed; though by some peculiar association he remembered canoeing at a summer camp near Blue Hill, Maine; afterwards (1921), he had puked at a clambake.

"Still don't want bats?" Clovis asked in a tiny voice.

Missus Fitzgerald, who could really keep her eye on the ball, said, "Nyao. And we don't want the tower either."

"Where's my breakfast?" roared Clovis.

"We want to live together," Ann addressed her mother. "Nicholas and I."

"How did you pick us?" Fitzgerald asked Clovis.

"I was looking for my foreman."

"Shut your little mouth," Missus Fitzgerald told her daughter, who gnawed fitfully at a sausage. Codd was at the door once again.

"Write my check," he said, "I've had the course."

"We'll talk about this after breakfast," Fitzgerald said to him. "You may be right."

"It's him or me," Codd said.

"Quite right," Fitzgerald said, "but later, okay? We'll have it all out."

"I'm old enough to make this decision," Ann told her mother. Codd went out. Clovis' breakfast came. He scowled at the lady of Amerind extraction who drummed around the table splashing cups full of coffee.

"What did you say?" Fitzgerald, this shocked man, asked his daughter.

"Nicholas and I wish to set up housekeeping."

"You just aren't fussy," her mother accused, "are you."

"And it's time she got started," Dad averred.

"Well, she's not, Duke. She's not fussy and she never was."

"Life has a way of bringing out fussiness."

"Ann," said her mother, "I hate to see you learn to be fussy the hard way."

"I told you later!" said Fitzgerald to Codd who had re-appeared. "Now get." Codd shrank away. "Not one bat tower," he said, catching Clovis' eye.

"I can get it for you cheap," Clovis said.

"Tell us you don't mean that," Missus Fitzgerald said.

"I don't mean that." Ann shrugged.

Now Clovis really began to eat as if there were no to-morrow, shooting through not only his own large breakfast, but all the leftovers as well. At one point, he had three pieces of toast and an unsqueezed grapefruit clamped in the appliance. It would be friendly and fun to say that he held the others in thrall.

Payne excused himself with the tiny wink that means the toilet; and escaped. The truth was the blood vessels in his head were pounding in an apoplectic surge. He went outside under the exploding cottonwoods and hot mountain light feeling an upwelling of relief of freedom of space of scarcity of knowing there was the invisible purling descent of mountain water someplace right close. In the watercourses on the side slope he could see green hands of aspen the million twirling leaves. Then he jumped into the Hornet and bolted.

A time-lapse photograph would have shown the palest mint-green band against the mountains and the steady showering of transcontinental earthclods from the dying rocker panels and perforated bulbosities of fender. Behind the spiraling lizard of glass-faults, the preoccupied face of him, of Payne. What did he ever do to anybody?

The man at the Texaco who had excited himself about the bushwhacked recaps said, "Go ahead and use it. Not long distance, we hope." Payne looked around. There was no one else. "We?"

"You and me."

"Oh, no, no, no, no just a local call."

A minute later, Payne asked Codd to give him Clovis. Clovis came to the phone.

"Hello?" he asked warily.

"Me, Payne. Get out of there. I don't want you peddling a tower to my future in-laws."

"Future in-laws. You ought to hear them on the subject of you, pal."

"I have and don't want to anymore."

"A horse who isn't gwine finish."

"I don't need to know that."

"Where are you?"

"The Texaco."

"Are you coming back ever?" So Clovis had picked up the true pitch of Payne's departure.

"The body says yes."

He'd been gone an hour. When he sat down at the table,

132

he could see the Fitzgeralds sniffing the Hornet's fuel leaks. Once Payne saw a picture of André Gide in his library, wearing a comfy skull cap, looking at a bound folio and puffing his Gauloise cigarette. Thinking of that now, Payne couldn't completely see why he should continue to take his lumps here in the presence of breakfast scraps and depleted grapefruits.

"We've been having an incredible conversation with your boss," Missus Fitzgerald said to him.

"Good," Payne said.

"About these oddities, these bat towers, you two are pushing."

"I'm just the simple carpenter," Payne said.

"Mister Clovis says you're going to Key West," said Fitzgerald, unnaturally elated to be able to announce this.

"It's news to me."

"Yup," Clovis grinned, "it's so. Are you ready for the rest?"

"I am."

"I nailed them for twenty G's: one tower and one only. Naturally, it will be our masterpiece." Payne was pleased with the news; though it pained him to have Clovis use his confidence tone in front of the Fitzgeralds. "One catch. No bats down there. We're going to have to bring our own. Just a detail. And you did hear me about the twenty G's."

"Yes," Payne winced. They conversed as though the room were empty of anyone but themselves.

"You shoulda seen the two-page telegrams I was whamming down there. You didn't know it but I composed the damn queries in that creekbottom. And you oughta seen my literary style. Right out of the adventurer William Beebe whose underwater footsteps I have always longed to trace through the atolls of Micronesia."

"What in the hell are you talking about?"

"Twenty thousand dollars," Clovis said, "and how we got them."

About the time that it became plain that Payne would not only clear out soon but perhaps—even if it was not plain to the Fitzgeralds—take Ann along with him, Codd began to conduct a curious delineation of his own plans all toward asking himself the question whether or not he was willing to go to the State Penitentiary at Deer Lodge and there to manufacture license plates for automobiles, all for the pleasure of busting Nicholas Payne down to size and, in some ultimate manner, *fix* him for good. The question was in the long run one that sprang from a fantasy of himself scuttling out of a low, dense bush, whirring almost invisible out of that bush with his speed, to hit Payne over the head with something of a single ball-peen density sufficient to prevent the rising of Payne again from the spot on anything but a litter for the deceased. He giggled with a thought of Payne afloat in brains and spinal fluid. R.I.P. if you think you deserve it because here's where God takes over! Wayne was a religious boy.

The relief Codd got at having developed a frame of action permitted him to enjoy, as he once always had, his little bunkhouse. On the shelf beside the Motorola, a blue flowerpot burst with poppies grown right from a Burpee's packet. That took tender loving care! His postcards, cowboy writing paper, electric cattleprod, wrap-around sunglasses, Model 94 Winchester 30–30, bathing suit (Roger Vadim model), Absorbine, Jr., truss and Philmore crystal set with loop antenna—were all carefully arrayed in the doorless closet next to the TV. His 4-H belt buckle, angora dice, birthday cards (30) from his grandmother and novelty catalogues were all on the dresser next to his great-grandfather's Confederate forage cap and great-grandmother's hard porcelain chamberpot out of which he had eaten untold tonnage of treated grains and cereals from the factories of Battle Creek, Michigan.

And on the walls were many varnished pine plaques emblazoned with mottos. And there were snapshots of girlfriends, bowling trophies, hot cars, a dead eagle spread over the flaring hood of a Buick Roadmaster. In the top right-hand dresser drawer behind the army socks were many unclear snapshots of Ann's twat. Seen from under the bathhouse floor by the impartial eye of the Polaroid camera, it seemed itself to be a small, vaguely alarming bird, not unlike a tiny version of the American eagle lying on the hood of the Buick Roadmaster; alarming to Codd anyway, who, let's face it, never had known what to make of it. What was the use of his getting a lot of pictures of the darn thing if he couldn't touch it?

The bed was just a bed. The chairs were just a bunch of chairs. There was a parabolic heater with black and white fabric cord. There was just a regular bunch of windows— well, only four; but they seemed to be all over the place. One window was close to the door and today it framed the blaring red mug of an unhappy Duke Fitzgerald.

"Come out here a minute, Wayne."

There was just one Wayne Codd in there and he came out.

"Sir?"

"Can't you do anything?"

"He hasn't given me a chance."

"He did night before last. I found you K.O.'d on his step."

"I got sucker-punched, sir."

"Well, Codd, I thought you'd have had your own stake in this."

"Sir?"

"I mean I don't know if you realize what he's got her doing."

A dish dropped and broke faintly in the main house.

"Oh, yes I do, sir," Codd said firmly, "I've seen them at it."

Fitzgerald waved his hands frantically in front of his face. "For God's sake Wayne." Wayne looked down at his boots, remembered Orion streaking up, the lash of trees. "I saw them, sir."

Hideously, Fitzgerald had an agonizing image of Payne as a kind of enormous iguana or monitor lizard, even the beating throat, in rut, over the vague creaminess of Ann. Suddenly, out of the generalized eroticism, he was back in the winter of 1911, lying on his Flexible Flyer on a hill in Akron, imaginatively pitting himself against a flying-V of naked women. He remembered their rubbery collision, the women writhing and squealing under his runners.

"Codd it's rough. Chemistry . . . changing times . . . God I don't know."

"But I will do the job, sir."

"Gee Wayne I do hope so. It's what he ought to have."

"Don't you worry your head, sir. He's going to have it." Codd began to choke a little with emotion at having proclaimed even in so veiled a fashion his dismal loyalty. He was without relations and nobody loved him. This was going to have to do.

"Ann," said her mother, "wouldn't you stay a minute?"

"Of course I will, Mother. You never—"

"I know I'm tiresome and maybe a . . . a little old." The smile. "But just this once."

"You never want me to stay! You want me to get going after meals. 'Why don't you get a move on?' you're always saying! I'd love to sit and talk a minute for crying out loud!"

Missus Fitzgerald fanned all that away, all that sass, all that fearful adolescent whatnot, all that chemistry.

"I'm going to make you a proposal."

The little furrow, only one now, between the tapered eyebrows; the delicately rouged beezer narrowed with the seriousness of it. Ann grew desperate. I'm only a kid, she thought, I want to hightail it; not this thing with papers. She wondered what it could mean anyway, feeling her chemicals boil up the neck of her Pyrex beaker. But the old lady looked bananas as she produced now a red vinyl portfolio with her lawyer's name, B. Cheep, Counselor-At-Law, in gold rubber on its handle. Out came the papers, business papers, girl; papers with which Missus Fitzgerald planned to make a serious obstacle to Nicholas Payne.

"These aren't only for people who go bald," said the Missus.

"What's this? What *is* this, Mother?"

"The wig bank! The wig bank!" The famous lapis lazuli glitter of eyes.

"Oh."

"You say 'oh.'"

"Actually, yes."

"I wonder if you would say, 'oh' in some of the circumstances I have been forced to visualize."

The gnomic tone bothered Ann.

"Maybe I would say something quite different, Mother."

"I wonder if you would say 'oh' if you were a part-time secretary at the bank in Wyandotte who had dropped December's salary on a teased blonde beehive which you had stored all through the summer and broken out for the Fireman's Ball in November only to find that the expensive article contained a real thriving colony of roaches and weevils; so you spray it with DDT or 2, 4-D or Black Flag or Roach-No-Mo and all the bugs, all the roaches, all the weevils run out and the wig bursts into flames by *spontaneous combustion* and the house which you and your hubby—because that's what they call their husbands, those people: *hubbies*—burns down around the wig and your nest egg goes up with the mortgage and it's the end. I wonder then, if you were her and had owned this wig which you had stored privately, I wonder if you would have wondered about a refrigerated fireproofed wig bank after all? Or not."

A little voice: "I would have put my wig in the wig bank."

"I THOUGHT SO. And I was wondering one last thing. I was wondering if the owner of this wig bank came up to you and hinted at a partnership I was wondering if you would shrug with that pretty little dumbbell face and say 'oh.'"

Suddenly Ann wanted to bring in the cane crop in Oriente Province where the work and earth was good all at once and Castro came out in the evenings to pitch a few innings and maybe give your tit a little squeeze and said he appreciated your loading all those *arrobas* for the people; and the cane fields ran to the sea where a primitive but real belief in Art helped people meet the day.

"How can I be your partner?" she asked.

"Come to Detroit with me now."

"But Nicholas I wanted to see more of Nicholas."

"You wanted to see more of Nicholas."

"Don't make fun."

"I had smaller chances for developing standards, my girl. But I developed them I assure you. I was fussy."

"Well, so am I."

"Not to my way of thinking."

"I'll go along with that."

"You control your tone," her mother said.

"You control yours."

"Trying to extort a half interest in my wig bank and not plan on showing up for the work side of things."

"I don't want a half interest in your little bitch of a wig bank."

"You don't have the standards for the job anyway," says the Ma, lighting a Benson and Hedges. "Well, you won't get it I assure you. We need people who are fussy." When Missus Fitzgerald got rolling scarcely anyone in sight got off unabraded.

Ann went to her room. She was comforted a little by it and by the tremendous number of familiar objects. But the objects themselves brought a special discomfort. In this way: Ann felt that it might soon be requisite for her to go with Payne someplace and she wanted to do that. But she wanted to stay around and play with all the junk in her room and look out of the window and read passionate books and write poems and take photographs that held meaning. And she didn't mind getting laid either if she could sleep at home; but to be out there on the road doing it and not be able to go back and play with all the junk at night. . . . Plus, someday, and this had to be gone into rather systematically, when it became necessary to think in terms of the long run, she did not want to find she had closed the door on George, the rara avis, as her father called him.

Payne knew the time was coming now. He didn't know when precisely; nor did he know that Wayne Codd, former Gyrene and present-day homicidal knucklehead extraordinaire, stalked him from afar, looking for an opening and feeling soundly backed up by the Fitzgeralds senior. Codd himself had no plan. He was just going to get in there and let the worst of his instincts take over. By contrast, Payne, excited about his coming travels, thought of the open roads of America and the *Saturday Evening Post* and its covers by his favorite artist besides Paul Klee: Norman Rockwell. "Make it me who's out there!" He saw spacious skies and amber waves of grain. Most of all he saw the alligator hammocks of Florida and, in his mind's eye, a stately bat tower standing in an endless saw-grass savannah over which passed the constant shadows of tropical cloudscapes; merry bats singled out stinging bugs at mealtime; Payne confronted a wall of Seminole gratitude. And on a high rounded beach the multiple amputee of original bat schemes smiled at a blue horizon.

You'd think he'd never been there.

These frosty mornings put the young wanderer in mind of the Tamiami Trail. He remembered, not uncritically, juice bars where the hookers went to keep up their vitamin C. He remembered a cocktail lounge with aquarium walls that let you see water ballet. He remembered his surprise when girls who had waited on him before appeared behind the glass, streams of bubbles going up from the corners of forced subaqueous smiles. Most of all, he remembered the vivid, rubbery cleavage of one of the girls who swam toward the glass. He wanted to stir her with wrinkled waterlogged fingers of his own. One day, he sat close to the glass and made a simian face over his cuba libre. The girl, who turned out to be a Seminole, laughed huge silver globes to the surface.

He was seventeen. Those were the days when he still went around on crutches for no reason at all and carried a pistol. He was riding his first motorcycle, an early hog, acetylene-torched from the contours of a Harley 74 ("Call

140

it a Harley cause it harley ever starts."), toward Everglades City with the Seminole girl on the back. For the first part of the ten days they traveled together, she seemed as assimilated as an airline stewardess—owned a bikini, ate snacks, screwed with a coy reserve and made, while doing so, the same "bleep" Payne heard subsequently from small weather satellites. He carried the crutches on the bike, the pistol in his pants. By the end of the trip, the coy reserve had vanished and in all respects, Payne felt, she had become an aborigine.

She taught him this: Hold the pistol at the ready, ride the back roads in the 'glades at night in first gear with the lights on dim; when you spot a rabbit, hit the brights, shift to second and "get on it a ton" until you overtake the rabbit, draw the gun, shoot the rabbit and stop.

Then the aborigine would skin the rabbit, make a fire and cook it over little flames that lit their faces, the motorcycle and the palmettos. After that, whiskey drinking and off-color games would set in.

One night she took him to see an alligator the poachers hadn't found: an enormous beauty with jaws all scarred from eating turtles. Miami wasn't far away; but this was a thousand years ago, back when the Harley was already old.

Now Payne meant to show Ann what it had been like. Incipient Calvinism would keep him from divulging the details of the Seminole girl's lessons. Historically, she would be simply an Indian who had guided him in the Everglades.

Payne had no way of knowing that Ann would expand his entire sense of the word "aborigine" with cute tricks of her own.

Codd was summoned to the library, scene of recent

ballpoint skirmishes and terminal conferences re: the transgressions of Payne. Missus Fitzgerald smoked contemplatively in the bay window, looking out upon the greedy willow that secretly probed for delicious effluents in the Fitzgerald septic tank. Fitzgerald, turned to the liquor wagon, his back to Codd, his hands doing something invisible like a baseball pitcher adjusting a secret grip on the ball. Abruptly he turned with one of his chunky famous highballs aloft for Codd—thinking, "The foreman is brought in for a drink with the owner"—and said, "Our dear Wayne."

Why not simply accept the fact that the willow is a symbol.

"Thank you," said Wayne.

"What do you think of this Payne?" asked Missus Fitzgerald.

"I dunno really."

"Go ahead," said Fitzgerald, "roll it over in your mind: What do you really think of the bastard."

"I've got my doubts," Codd said.

Missus Fitzgerald chuckled. "You're so deferential, Wayne. That makes us even fonder of you." Wayne thought of automotive differentials, how they accepted the power of the motor and made those wheels turn massively like all those wheels turned massively in grade-school educational movies about the U.S. on the go.

"Wayne," said Fitzgerald, "we've got our doubts as well. But because of Ann, who is essentially just a baby still, can you follow that? still just a baby, Wayne, because of Ann this guy has us over a barrel and we have no recourse at all. He cannot be discouraged. He cannot be sent away. God, I remember when I was wooing the missus, why hell I—"

"Let's not talk about you just now, dear."

"That's right, honey. Let's keep our eye on the ball. —Uh, Wayne, I don't know how to say this—" He turned to his wife. "—but God damn it honey, aren't we getting fond of Wayne?"

Wayne picked up the thread right along in here, about how he was earmarked as the son-in-law. In his mind's eye, he twirls a silk opera hat; beside him in the box, Ann listens raptly as a heavy fellow in a jerkin bays, *"Amour!"*

"Yes, Duke, indeed we are."

"Wayne, let me throw the meat on the table. This bird has kind of got the double whammy on us, what with Ann's being, at this point, little more than a child. And, on the level, the guy has our hands tied."

"This goes way back," says Missus Fitzgerald. "We've had him in the house like a cat burglar, you know, rooting through the liquor cabinet and whatnot." Fitzgerald studied her face for indiscretion. "No, Duke, now," she said, seeing it. "Wayne has to know."

"This is true," Duke acceded slowly.

"Anyhow, we just wanted to fill you in," she said.

"Kind of put the bee in your bonnet," he said.

"And you kind of see what you can come up with," she said.

"Go ahead and finish your highball," he said.

"You've hardly touched it," she said.

"Oh, hell, take it to the bunkhouse and finish it," he said. "And bring back the glass when you're through."

14

C. J. Clovis too was now asleep in the mobile home; he had removed the two artificial limbs. Since the missing arm and missing leg were from the same side of his body, he looked, sleeping on his stomach, like a boomerang. In his dreams, he twitched with happiness. He saw his towers crossing the country, none out of sight of the other. He dreamed of a natural harmony in which the silent war of bats on bugs left a ground level peace where ladies shelled peas under evening trees. Slivers of white showed between his lids as his eyes rolled to applause.

Two years ago, George published Ann's poems. It was a birthday present. The book was reviewed in *Sumac*, a literary magazine which had assumed the subscription list of a former publication, *Diesel*, a journal of lesbian apologetics. Seeing the review again gave Ann such a sense of her own ability to synthesize hard-edge experience that she lost a good deal of her fear of going off with Nicholas:

. .

It is difficult to talk of the work of Ann Fitzgerald without mentioning the sense of longing, of time and love past, that percolates through her best verse. These are delicate moods that survive the most concrete—even brutal—details. This, from *A Loss Of Petals* (George Russell Editions, Malaga, 1968):

> "Beside me on *our* bed
>   his sleep fitful:
> We *lingered* at our lovemaking(s).
>
> And at his tossings
>   his
>   dong
>   flopped
>   wanly
> To the Posturepedic shadows
>   of mice and loss."

At a time when poetry faces schism and a dearth of real gift, Fitzgerald's perfect reveries throb just under the skin of a discredited craft.

She would have shown the book to Payne long ago, if it hadn't been for the publisher's colophon. And she didn't really want him to know how clever she was. Moreover, she had a specific interest in photographing him when he was being most emptily superior, when reflex maleness made him show himself at his worst. Nothing personal, mind you; she was chasing universals.

In the immediate future, she wanted only a dead-level view of the country. She wanted to be along for the ride just like those cowboy's floozies she saw at all hours sitting under the rear-view mirrors of pickups. The simple national archetypes like floozies, bowlers and rotarians seemed suddenly to be rather at one with things, possibly in a way Lozenge could never have foreseen. In an epoch in which it was silly to be a druid or red Indian, there was a certain zero-hour solace in being something large enough to attract contempt. Ann looked forward to being a floozy as another girl might have anticipated her freshman year at Vassar. With almost Germanic intentness, she had set her sights on being cheap and available and not in the least fussy.

She broke out the peroxide, pouted at herself in the mirror and squeaked, "Call me Sherri."

In the quiet of a Michigan evening, Payne's mother tweezed a dog's hair from the meat loaf. A moment later, without warning, she thrust a spoiled cheese into a lidless plastic garbage pail. Payne's father, in the den, stared at a picture of Payne dribbling in for a lay-up. "Mother," he called to Missus Payne, who was trying apparently to thrust that cheese all the way to the bottom of the pail. "Here's that picture of Nicholas dribbling in for a lay-up you asked about!"

Nicholas Payne hunkered in his handmade bow-roofed and screened motor wagon and packed with joy his possessions. He knew that this little driveway he was parked in was hooked up to every road in America; and all those roads ran to the sea.

He slowly packed his mummy bag into its stuff sack thereby closing the parenthesis on whatever fantasies he had had about walking over the mountains that summer. He took the sheepherders' stove to pieces and stored it. He lifted the cookware down from the hooks on the ceiling and rolled the Coleman lantern in a towel.

· ·

Wayne Codd sat on the one-front step that his bunkhouse had, watched Payne, and waited for it to get dark. He just wanted to get in there and play it by ear. Afterwards—on those evenings when he and Ann weren't at the opera—they would have two possibly three *hand-picked* couples over for bridge and drinks. Sometimes when they were feeling restless, they would drive out to Gallatin Field to see the kind of people who got off the plane, just to keep a check on that. Late that night, Ann would perform her duties as a wife. Codd troubled over that idea a moment or two, mistakenly emphasizing the word "perform" in his mind; until with exquisite anguish he saw what was essential to the notion. "*Duties!*" he groaned with ecstasy. "*Perform duties!*"

Dad Fitzgerald was awfully hungry and just prowling around the kitchen and getting in the Missus' way. She ignored him and moved through the room with a certain dirigible grace. When, from time to time, he caught her eye they smiled at each other; until once when he smiled and she just stared back at his face. She came up close to him. "I thought so," she said. "Get back upstairs and groom your nose!"

"I'm hungry!"

"I'm not going to have that at dinner. I told you if you let yourself go I'd go back for bank inventory. Now groom that nose." Fitzgerald started to leave the room. Her voice softened. "Dinner will be ready when you come down," she added to placate the honking auto dodo.

He went back up the stairs of a house built on the ancestral hunting grounds of the Absaroka Indians, with a gloomy certainty that the rotary nose clipper had been left at home. And even though he knew it was irrational, he began to lose interest in the West.

Codd, originally hunkered by the wagon, later hunkered by a bush; and then out of pure feral instinct, moved, unconsciously, under the bush itself until his camouflage was quite complete and only the shiny points of his Mariposa cowboy boots and slow-burn eyes would have been visible to a botanist peering to identify the bush (Juniper).

The point of his left elbow rested upon his knee. His left hand supported his face, tilted to the left to smear slightly the flesh on the Anglo-Mongol cheekbone. His right forearm rested upon the other knee at such a pitch that his finger dangled all the way to the ground, resting delicately upon the end of an iron sash weight.

If you had photographed Codd and drawn a circle around the picture of him, the diameter of which was a direct line drawn from the tip of one boot to the crown of his head, he would have filled the whole circle with the rest of his body; he was compact, in this posture, as dense and raring as a seamless cannonball.

No one photographed Codd. No one knew Codd was in the bush with the sash weight watching Payne behind the screen of his wagon. Codd could see little more than the movement of a lantern now behind the screens and behind the leaves of his own bush. Rising over the barn in a sky still very slightly blue, the moon made a mark like when your arm is grabbed and a fingernail sinks. A light was still on in the barn. The door was open and a luminous gold rectangle of hay dust was lit from behind. Codd was passing time by guessing weights and distances. As patient and systematic as he seemed to be, Wayne Codd was in the most important ways completely out of kilter. The words "ball peen" pivoted through his mind too ardently for anyone's comfort but his own.

Payne examined the trailer hitch with a flashlight. It was a good sturdy mount with welded struts and a two-inch ball. The trouble was it was necessarily attached to the car. He could see the circle of metal corruption around each of the welds and, looking underneath, whole sections of the frame seemed mechanically compromised and degenerate. The essential horridness of the Hudson was disclosing itself. It had begun to destruct.

He crawled further under the car, examining the places where the steel of the springs had crystallized. The shocks were hopeless. Every grease nipple exuded a fist of gritty sludge. As Payne looked around, he began to develop a fear that the car would collapse on top of him.

How he wished he had his old Matchless motorcycle again with its single 500 c.c. cylinder, its low-end monster torque and simplicity. He was sick of the lurching mechanical hysteria. He wanted to stretch out on the Matchless, his chin on the gas tank, his feet crisscrossed on the rear fender, his hands out in front of him like a man in a racing dive, and listen to that English engine come up on the cam for the purest and most haunting wail he had ever heard since Niña de los Peines.

No more Hudson Hornet seat springs liberating suddenly from the long oppression of upholstery to stick him in the ass. No more steel shriek of brakes and sudden vision of highway through the floorboards. No more gradual twirl of rear-view mirror or wide-open charge down quiet streets even though the foot was off the accelerator and he was now groping on the floor to pull it back.

Payne wanted a Coupe de Ville with mink upholstery.

He wanted factory air and four on the floor. He wanted tinted glass and the optional four barrels. He wanted a stingy-brim Stetson and a twenty-three-hair moustache. He wanted the AM–FM with stereo speakers in the back, the tape deck; and the climate control lever that let you have Springtime in the Laurentians forever.

For a long time he lay there with the nine-battery Ray-O-Vac in his hand. It never occurred to him that it was unwieldy and flimsy compared to a sash weight.

Codd saw the light fan out from under the car and started to make his move. He spilled forward onto his fingertips, his face up and forward like a mandril's; and sidled into the evening air.

During the Livingston rodeo, a gopher and a rattlesnake had faced off under one Engelmann's spruce way up in the ultraviolet-saturated shadows of the Absarokas. Only the snake had been able to pay attention. After that the gopher was done for. A goner. What's more, the gopher died a virgin. His own secret genetic message sent a million years ago went undelivered. The message of the snake, however, had gone special-handling first-class registered. Which goes to show: It doesn't pay to scrimp on postage.

Payne was remembering when the dogs were passing the foot of the stairs. Is that what they were? Were they dogs? Yes, he decided, those were man's best friends passing the foot of the stairs. Sometimes he feared going downstairs in the morning that they'd still be there to rip through his terrycloth robe and tear at his inwards.

He looked at the rather vague edge of the Hornet's rocker panel. Thrust under and toward him were the snakeskin tips of Wayne Codd's Mariposa cowboy boots.

Payne understood now. He imperceptibly moved the

flashlight off his chest and propped it beside him so that it continued to fan out at exactly the same angle. Codd's placement of his feet, just outside the penumbra of light, now made sense. Then Payne moved carefully to get out from under the car at the other side. He looked back. The boots hadn't moved. The long curves of them were criss-crossed with the shadows of tie-rods. Payne rolled free, rising slowly to look at Codd through the windows of the car. Codd's head was bent downward, watching with absolute attention and lack of motion.

As yet, Payne had not specified his alarm, picked his flavor between terror and concern. He moved very cautiously to the front of the car without alerting Codd and then watched him for some moments. He spotted the long billet of sash and felt an indignation of his own that was entirely dangerous. He studied Codd very closely then. He could not have missed anything. He did not miss the soundless motion of Codd's eyes turning up to see him.

Codd began to move, loose and righteous with what he had to do. When he was close enough he swung at Payne. He swung too far because the weighted fist hit Payne under the ear so that Payne felt something sing through him but did not fall. Then, when Codd missed on the next swipe and kicked wildly at Payne, Payne rushed him and got him over the hood of the car battering him against the moonlit dihedral of windshield and feeling a tremendous turbulence inside of himself as he lifted the ragdoll weight of the shrieking Codd up again and again to beat him full length over the front of the car. And, as though Codd were without any weight at all, he began to no longer hear Codd striking the car but could only see the head as fragile as a winter melon colliding against the curving glow of glass making spidery shooting stars in the windshield at every touch.

Payne released him, sickened, and sat down. Fitzgerald was in full motion running toward him, crossing and re-crossing the rectangle of light from the barn. Then Ann was coming too, an enormous silver nimbus of bleached hair around her head.

In complete physical possession, Payne watched the lolling go out of Codd's head as he came down from the hood of the car. Codd seemed a moment later to teeter back from the angle of the Mariposa boots as he raised the sash weight high overhead and brought it down against Payne's skull. Payne felt himself guide its clear descent with his eye. The moment of shock was a single click, as a cue ball touches the triangle of billiard balls, a clean line, a perfect sound, then the balls of color bursting from the center and darkness pouring in until zero.

15

It was quickly apparent that Codd had not given Payne, as it first looked, a blow that was mortal. The question of damage to the brain, however, was not settled. The notion Ann had was that her family would take an upright line in compensating Nicholas. As for herself, she would feel honor bound to do whatever he told her to do.

Now that was an alarming idea. She was filled with a terrifying and delicious vision of living her life out with a man who had been made a feeb by damage to his brain. She saw her parents out of misguided loyalty giving Payne work that he could do. And suddenly a terrible picture of Payne wheeling bins of disinfected wigs in her mother's wig bank came to Ann. For a long time, she had secretly photographed Payne at his worst moments; but pictures of him reduced to idiocy by brain damage would be of merely pathological, rather than artistic, interest. This thought of hers, clear as it was, diminished Ann more than she would ever be able to know.

But, poor girl, she was so undermined at the moment. At the time of the accident, she had seen the complicity between Codd and her parents; one, she assumed, that had got out of hand. Then her mother had spotted Ann's peroxide hair and, even before it was determined whether or not Payne was dead, had screeched, "You little hoor!"

When Payne regained consciousness, he discovered that he had lost much of his peripheral vision; producing what the doctor described as "vignetting"; it gave him the sense of looking down a pair of tubes. Added to the insane headache he had, it was very disconcerting. No one knew if it was permanent or not.

Ann came often but he could never quite figure if he had just seen her or imagined it. So he lay there in an indescribable air of expectation, most of which turned out to be unwarranted.

Clovis was in and out all the time, displaying his familiarity with the staff. He gave Payne some advice that seemed rather wild-eyed in the beginning and then made sense. Clovis conducted a few arrangements to substantiate the advice and, two days later, Payne was feeling well enough to act upon it.

Summoned by Payne's attorney, sitting beside him now, the Fitzgeralds arrived at the hospital, all three of them. Payne directed them to chairs and they sat, next to the sink.

"As soon as I am able," Payne said, "I am going to Key West to build a bat tower. I plan to take Ann with me. We will of course live together; 'cohabit' is the word, Heath informs me." Payne gestured to indicate Counselor Egdon Heath beside him. "Both on the way and after we get there."

"I'm afraid that won't be possible," La smiled, boiled eggs for eyes. "We don't operate that way."

154

"Fill them in, Heath."

Heath ingratiated himself with a suggested, if not actual, undulance and a winning meringue smile. The Fitzgeralds were thrown into ghastly discomfort. "There are any number of writs we can serve you with at this time," he began. "I have advised my client to pursue an individual suit in the amount of two millions. Mister Payne has a fetching inability to speculate in terms of such numbers. So I showed him the tax assessor's rather conservative estimate of the value of your ranch and assured my client there would be quite a bit of change left over! I do not hint at avarice by any means when I say that this procedure has had the effect of piquing Mister Payne's interest. And of course we have not given up the notion of going for the wig bank as well. My own point of view is based on the fact that I am here on speculation. And it costs me twenty thousand dollars a week to leave my office in Los Angeles.

"Furthermore . . . a mint?" They shook their heads. He ate one, palming the foil. "Furthermore, a Mister Wayne Codd, temporarily resident in the fearful little city, has signed his name to half a dozen statements of his own composition. My evaluation is that they hint at a criminal dimension to this affair that could be explored with a mind to not only cleaning you out but salting you away!" He muttered insincerely to himself that he must abjure the vernacular, then cried, "Acky poo! I know how you feel about that! In the beginning, I didn't see why I should leave Los Angeles. I just didn't. But there was something that turned me on. Something that thrilled me and I searched it out. I lay in my Barcalounger until it came. And it turned out that it was the fact that we had both punitive and compensatory options in prosecuting this suit that gave me, frankly, a kind of hard-on to repre-

155

sent this man." Then Heath admitted to his voice a dry Episcopal scorn he had learned many years before at the Cranbrook School for Boys.

"Mister Payne has made me promise to say this: He will call me off in the event your daughter goes to Florida not only unhindered but without disapproval expressed through inheritance provisos." Heath was counting on a certain Republican solidity in the Fitzgeralds to keep his case airtight.

"We will not be blackmailed," one or possibly both of the Fitzgeralds said firmly.

"Presumably not," said Heath, "and that point of view fills me with pleasure. I personally never expected you to sell your daughter down the river in quite the manner indicated here."

"Heath," Payne said, "you're chiseling."

"Quite right."

"I told you I wouldn't have any of your damn greediness," Payne said. Heath was chastised.

"You're absolutely correct," he said; he could afford this. Payne had the opposition dead to rights.

"I suggest you drop everything you've said," Missus Fitzgerald announced, looking at the ceiling with a bored recitative air, "while you still have something left."

"There's nothing more to add, madame," said Heath, not only a lawyer, husband and father, but an influential man who had given Los Angeles Episcopalianism its particular sheen. "You know how it stands. I assume we begin suit. Do contact your own attorney immediately; and be sure he's good." Frivolous imitations of generosity by Egdon Heath.

"I should have thought your investigations would demonstrate that we have effective counsel," said Missus Fitzgerald, her words and words only having any conviction.

156

Fitzgerald himself broke in, chuckling to himself for quite some time. "You lawyers have tickled me for years. You're all pork-and-beaners till the day you die. I don't care if you make a million a day."

"Go ahead. You're bagged. Get in a speech."

"May I go on, Mister Heath? I was saying I really have to chuckle—" He showed how you do. "—when I think of you guys. You never get the human underpinning into your heads. You're constantly trotting out your writs and enjoinders without ever seeing that the law is a simple extension of the most ordinary human affairs."

"That's not true. Go ahead."

"May I continue, Mister Heath?"

"Do that. But you're bagged and bagged big."

"May I go on you fucking shyster?"

"Duke!"

"Daddy!"

"Wildly and emotionally inaccurate. But go on."

Fitzgerald composed himself and said, "What you as a particular lawyer have missed in this particular instance expresses perfectly what I am saying." Fitzgerald sat on his triumph like a jocular playmate. "Our daughter has already expressed a wish to go off with Mister Payne!" Missus Fitzgerald joined the fun of a smiling triumph directed at this L.A. pinhead.

"I know that," said Heath simply.

"Then what's the problem?" one or possibly both of the Fitzgeralds asked at once.

"You said she couldn't go," Heath said with even greater simplicity.

"Your small sense of conduct surprises us in a professional man of law," said Missus Fitzgerald. "Any parent would recognize our refusal as a way mothers and fathers have of stalling for time while they make up their minds."

Her pronunciation of the words "mother" and "father" was straight out of Dick And Jane. The Fitzgeralds looked at each other. They were winging it together, depending now on their intimacy, their knowledge of each other. This would be a test of what their marriage was founded upon.

"We have decided," said Mister Fitzgerald, looking hopefully at his bride, "that Ann is old enough to make her own decisions. In this case—" Oh, this was beautiful. "—we definitely do *not* approve of her decision."

"But will you stand in her way?" Heath, out of control, pleaded.

"No."

"What! You're opening the door to lewdness!"

"Heath," Payne warned.

"She's a grown woman," Missus Fitzgerald insisted.

Heath began to shout: "There's a question of consortium here, God damn it! It is technically questionable if these people have a right to intercourse. And without that legal right they are fornicators! You call yourself *parents* in the face of this abrogation of decency!"

Payne: "Shut up, Heath. Shut up and get out."

Heath ignored him. "A minor distrainment of your chattels and you sell your child into bondage! Let me ask you one thing. Let me ask you this. Have you questioned the effect of bastardy on the esteem you doubtless hold in your community? I mean, what if there is illegitimate issue? What if there is?"

Payne lay on his side now holding his head. The others were rigid with horror as the white-knuckled L.A. shyster circled them sinfully. "Let us talk reason. Exemplary or punitive damages in this action are extremely unlikely, right? The community has no need to make an example of you. Do you follow me? In equity, the assessment of damages is wholly within the discretion of the court where you will be more likely to get sympathetic treatment than my client. I mean, look at him. He looks like a crackpot. My client is everybody's fantasy of an ambulatory anarchist. Isn't he yours? Ask yourself that.

"Now lastly—and try to get this straight—it is the plaintiff's responsibility to keep damages to the minimum indicated by the tort. In this instance, the multiple of damages actually sustained is difficult to specify.

"I advise that you settle out of court. I advise that you keep your daughter in the home in which she belongs."

"How much?" Fitzgerald asked.

"I'm thinking of a hundred grand."

"The hell with that noise," Fitzgerald said and walked, his wife beside him, with dignity from the room. They would have to buy some champagne and celebrate their victory.

Ann delayed. She leaned over Payne's bed and filled Payne's ear with hot breath when she said, "They've sold me down the river, darling. It's you and me now." She left.

On his own way out, Egdon Heath said, somewhat acidly, to Payne, "I ought at least to nail you for my air fare."

"That's the life of a speculator," Payne said. "Nice try."

Payne was whacked out. He made friends with the nurse who attended him. She had tiny close-set eyes and an upturned bulbous nose. She told Payne her life story pausing upon occasion to break into tears. She had remained unwed through her thirties; then suddenly married an elderly motorist from a nearby town. Recently he told her that it had not in the least been love at first sight. So there was that for her to cry about. Payne took her hand, seeing her face at the end of a tube, and told her, "Don't sweat it, darling," in his most reassuring glottal baritone.

They didn't do a thing to Payne but take one kind of reading or another, including an X-ray. They took readings day after day. "What's my temperature?" Payne would ask. Or, "What's my pulse?" Or, "What's my blood pressure?" One day, sleepily, he inquired, "What numbers am I, Doctor?"

"Quite a few," the doctor said. "All of us are."

One thing Payne thought of continually was the time he blasted the piano with his .22, the beautiful splintering of excessively finished wood, the broken strings curling away from liberated beams of spicy piano light, the warm walnut stock of his .22, the other spice of spent shells, the word hollowpoint, the anger of the enemy, the silver discs the bullets made on the window, the simple precision of a peep sight, the blue of barrel steel, the name Winchester when you were in America, the world of BB Caps, Shorts, Longs, and Long Rifles, the incessant urge to louse up monuments, even the private piano monument he perforated from a beautiful tree with an almost blinding urgent vision of the miserable thing ending in an uproar of shattered mahogany, ivory, ebony and wire. No more Bach chords to fill the trees with their stern negation. There's no room here for a piano, he remembered righteously. No pianos here please.

Ann sat in the front of the Hudson. Just as in the songs, she had hair of sparkling gold and lips like cherry wine. Perhaps, hair of sparkling pewter and lips the color of a drink called Cold Duck. She looked like an awful floozy. Her eyes had melting antimony edging on their lids. God

160

only knew what she had in mind. She looked as round-heeled as a tuppeny upright after ten years of throwing standing crotch locks on every womb worm that came her way.

His vision, however, had improved; to the effect that the world no longer appeared as a circular vista at the end of a conduit. His urge to ride on the highway was now a quiet, tingling mania.

"Let us hear from you," the Fitzgeralds said when the kissing had stopped.

"Sure will," Ann said, "I'll drop you a line one of these days." Her parents looked at her. They needed the right word and quick. Something had gone entirely dead here.

"Let us know if you need anything," her mother tried.

"Yeah, right." Payne started to back around. "Take it easy," Ann said. And they left.

"I guess," Ann said after they had driven a while, "it had gotten to be time for me to cut out."

"All right," Payne said, "now take it easy."

"Darling, I'm upset."

"Yes, me too. My head is all fouled up."

"I feel like a hoor," she said. Payne felt a distant obligation to contradict her.

They passed through the box canyon of the Yellowstone where the venturi effect of chinook winds will lift a half-ton pickup right to the top of its load leveler shocks and make the driver think of ghost riders in the sky until the springs seat again and the long invisible curves of wind unknit and drive him through the canyon as though his speed were laid on him as paint.

Some hours later, Ann seemed to have fallen into a bad mood. "Where are we going?"

"Bat country," said Payne. That quieted her down.

"You know what?" she asked later.

"What?"

"This damn car of yours is coming off on my clothes."

At Apollinaris Spring, Ann thought: My God, if George ever saw me pull a low-rent trick like this! In fact that's something to think about. She began to record the voyage with her camera.

They dropped down into Wyoming and headed for Lander, running through implausible country where Sacajawea and Gerald McBoingBoing fought for the table scraps of U.S.A. history.

Coming down through Colorado, still west of the Divide, they passed a small intentional community—people their own age—all of whose buildings were geodesic domes made of the tops of junked automobiles. Payne could see gardens, a well, a solar heater and wanted to go down. But the members of the community were all crowding around down there and rubbing each other. They were packing in down there and Payne felt the awful shadow of the Waring Blender and drove on. Ann was mad. "Why won't you mix, God damn it?" I read Schopenhauer, Payne thought, *that tease!*

They headed for Durango, stayed for a day, then dropped into New Mexico and headed for Big Spring, Texas.

They cut across Amarillo and made a beeline for Shreveport on a red-hot autumn day to Columbia, Florida, where Payne had been sent in the first place by Cletus James Clovis. This was bat country. Payne took a piece of paper out of his pocket. A short time later, he was knocking on the door of a reconditioned sharecropper's house.

When the man opened the door, Payne saw the wall behind covered with curing gator skins. "C. J. Clovis said to see you about bats," Payne said. The poacher told them to come in and have something cool to drink.

A day later, Payne, with his biggest hang-over ever, and his companion, the poacher Junior Place, with a big one of his own; and Ann snoozing in the Hornet with an actual puker of a white lightning hang-over and her peroxide beehive full of sticks and bits of crap of one description or another, and the North Florida sun coming in like a suicide; the men paused at the end of the sandy road in the palmettos beside a pile of wrecked automobiles each of which held a little glass-and-metal still—the product of which drew a considerably better price locally than any bonded sauce you could find out at your shopping plaza. Payne was flattered at this confidential disclosure.

They had little distance to go. Junior had loaned Payne a pair of his own snakeproof pants—citrus picker's trousers with heavy-gauge screen sewn inside a canvas sleeve from the knee down. And the two of them crossed the palmettos on a gradually upward incline, near the crest of which Junior Place began to scout back and forth for the mouth of the cave.

He told Payne to feel as best he could for a breeze. So Payne wandered the crest of the hill, feeling for a breeze that came to him shortly as a breath of something cool and watery, something subterranean rising around him. He found the entrance in a cluster of brush from which a solid cool shaft of air poured. He called out its location.

The two men carried triangular nets on long hardwood poles. Payne had his nine-battery Ray-O-Vac and Junior Place carried a carbide lamp. Junior came over and pushed aside the brush to reveal a coal-black oval in the ground, a lightless hole through which he slid as from long practice.

It proves one thing about Payne that he followed straightaway. He wanted to maintain voice contact. "How do you know C. J. Clovis?"

"Hardly know him a tall," said Place. There was no way of knowing the immensity of this blackness; it sucked away Payne's voice without an echo.

There were things going by his head at tremendous speed. "I had a five-minute talk with the man," said Place. "He is a freak of nature." The blackness pressed Payne's face. "I'd do anything in the world for him. Come up side of me now. Okay, use the lamp." The lights went on. The paleness of the limestone hall surprised and terrified Payne. The colliding planes of wall and ceiling appeared serene and futuristic and cold. Every overhead surface was festooned with bats. They were all folded, though some, alive to the presence of the men, craned around; and a few dropped and flew squeaking crazily through the beams of light. Then a number more came down, whirled through the room with the others; and as if by signal they all returned to the ceiling.

They set the lights where they would give them advantageous illumination; and with the long-handled nets commenced scraping pole-breaking loads from the ceiling. A million bats exploded free and circulated through the chamber in a crescendo of squeaking. They upended the bats in the plastic mesh bags and continued swiping over head. By now, they needed only to hold the nets aloft and they would fill until they could not be held overhead.

Bats poured at Payne like jet engine exhaust; pure stripes and curves of solid hurtling bats filled the air to saturation. The rush and squeaking around Payne were making him levitate. As when the dogs were in the house,

164

he no longer knew which way his head or feet were pointing. He had no idea where the entrance was. Junior Place continued at the job, a man hoeing his garden. Payne whirled like a propeller.

When it was over, Payne had to be led out of the cave, carrying his net and shopping bag. There was an awful moment as the entrance began to pack all around him with escaping bats. When he finally stood outside the hole, he watched a single, towering black funnel, its point at the hole, form and tower over him.

He would have to tell Clovis: a tower actually made of bats.

They liberated the bats in the wagon behind the Hudson. The bats circulated, a wild squeaking whirlwind, before sticking to the screen sides to squeak angrily out at the men. Some of the bats, their umbrella wings partially open, crept awkwardly around the bottom of the wagon before clinging to the screened sides. Soon a number of them were hanging from the roof adaptably.

"Do you have any idea what a hang-over is like in the face of that?" Ann asked the two men.

They said goodbye to Junior Place at the end of the road. Payne returned the pants, gingerly fishing his own from the wagon.

Ann slumped against him and fell asleep once more. Place, at the end of his white lightning road, waved a straw hat and held his nets overhead at the edge of a palmetto wilderness in his snakeproof pants.

Payne aimed the load for Key West.

> I got ten four gears
> And a Georgia overdrive.
> I'm takin little white pills
> And my eyes is open wide. . . .

16

They woke up in the morning in the sleeping bag beside the car. The bats were running all over the wire. They already knew Payne was the one who fed them: banana and bits of dessicated hamburger.

Across a wet field in the morning in the peat smell of North Central Florida and surrounded by a wall of pines stood a rusting, corrugated steel shed with daylight coming through its sides variously. From one end, the rear quarters of a very large field mule projected; and the animal could be heard cropping within. On the broad corrugated side of the shed itself in monstrous steamboat letters, filigree draining from every corner,

FAYE'S
GIFT
SHOPPE

Payne fed the bats and started coffee on the camp stove while, her hair teased into something unbelievable, Ann shot over to Faye's. By the time the coffee was ready, she was back at the car with long gilt earrings hanging from her ears. "Check these," she said. "Wouldn't they be great for when we went dancing?"

"They would be that."

They could have made the Keys by nightfall. But Ann wanted to stop at a roadhouse near Homestead where she played all the Porter Wagoner, Merle Haggard, Jeannie C. Riley, Buck Owens and Tammy Wynette records on the jukebox and danced with a really unpromising collection of South Florida lettuce-pickers and midcountry drifters. Then Payne got too drunk to drive; so they slept one more night on the road at the edge of the 'glades with the bats squeaking and wanting to fly in the dark, wanting to go someplace, and Payne remembering in a way that made him upset the aborigine of ten years before.

In his liquor stupefaction—and rather woozy anyway from the tropic sogginess and the streaked red sky and the sand flies and mosquitoes and the completely surprising softness of the air and the recent memory of the yanking jukebox dancing—he was just a little alarmed by Ann's ardor at bedtime. She had the camera within reach and he was afraid she would pull something kinky. And then he was just detached from everything that was happening to him; so that he saw, as from afar, Ann commit a primitive oral stimulation of his parts. Engorged, frankly, as though upon a rutabaga, her slender English nose was lost in a cloud of pubic hair. They had the sleeping bag open, underneath the wagon, in case it rained. Ann detected Payne's reserve and aggressively got atop of him, hauling at his private. There was so little room that each time her buttocks lifted, they bumped the underside of the wagon and sent the bats surging and squeaking overhead. She facetiously filled the humid evening with Wagnerian love grunts.

They hit A1A heading down through Key Largo, the mainland becoming more and more streaked with water and the land breaking from large to small pieces until finally they were in the Keys themselves, black-green mangrove humps stretching to the horizon and strung like beads on the highway. Loused up as everything else in the country, it was still land's end.

"What do you think you're doing?" Payne finally asked.

Ann turned a face to him as expressionless as a pudding under the glued, brilliant hair.

"What do I think I'm doing?" she repeated as though to a whole roomful of people.

On either side, the serene seascapes seemed to ridicule the nasty two-lane traffic with monster argosy cross-country trucks domineering the road in both directions. From time to time, in the thick of traffic problems, Payne would look off on the pale sand flats and see spongers with long-handled rakes standing in the bows of their wooden boats steering the rickety outboard motors with clothes-line tied to their waists. Then below Islamorada he saw rusty trailers surrounded by weedy piles of lobster traps, hard-working commercial fishermen living in discarded American road effluvia.

In Marathon, a little elevation gave him the immensity of the ocean in a more prepossessing package—less baby blue—and he saw what a piss-ant portion of the terraqueous globe the land really is. They stopped to eat and Payne had turtle. The end of that street was blocked with the jammed-in immense bows of four shrimpers. Their trawling booms were tangled overhead. He could read *Southern Cross, Miss Becky, Tampa Clipper* and *Witchcraft*. On the deck of the *Tampa Clipper*, a fisherman in a wooden chair, his hat pulled over his eyes, and half-awake, gave the finger to a lady who sighted him through the view finder of her Kodak. When she gave up, his arm fell to the side of the chair, his head settled at an easier angle. He was asleep.

Suddenly, they were in the middle of Key West and lost with a wagonload of bats lurching behind them in side streets where it was hard to make a turn in the first place. They passed the Fifth Street Baptist Church and read its motto on a sign in front:

> WHERE FRIENDLINESS IS A HABIT
> AND PARKING IS NOT A PROBLEM.

They ran into the old salt pond and had to backtrack. They cut down Tropical Avenue to Seminary Street down Seminary to Grinnell out Grinnell to Olivia and down Olivia to Poorhouse Lane where they got the car jammed and had to enlist the neighborhood; who helped until they got a good look and backed off, saying, *"Bats!"*

But suddenly Payne was happy to be in Key West. It was Harry Truman's favorite town and Harry Truman was fine by Payne. He liked Truman's remark about getting out of the kitchen if you couldn't stand the heat. Payne thought that beat anything in Kierkegaard. He also liked Truman's Kansas City suits and essential Calvinized watchfob insouciance of the pre-Italian racketeer. He enjoyed the whole sense of the First Lady going bald while the daughter wheedled her way onto the Ed Sullivan show to drown the studio audience in an operatic mud bath of her own devising.

They went past the cemetery, the biggest open space in Key West, filled with above-ground crypts, old yellow-fever victims, the sailors of the *Maine*, as well as the ordinary dead, if you could say that.

169

Ann sneered at everything, though she had acquired, quite without irony, a rural accent.

"What is this act?" Payne asked, as if his own attempts to extrapolate the land through mimicry of its most dubious societal features were not absurd.

But Ann just watched the beautiful wooden houses go by; each, it seemed, separated from the other by a vacant lot full of moldering and glittering trash or by small, rusting car gardens with clumps of expired fantasies from the ateliers of Detroit.

To Ann, at that moment, America said one beautiful thing after another.

To Payne it said, *I got all pig iron.*

"Which way to Mallory Square?"

"Keep going."

They kept going and hit the Thompson–O'Neill shrimp docks.

They went thataway. From afar, the anodized fantasm of the Dodge Motor Home was peerlessly evident. It sat under the quasi-Moorish battlements of the First National Bank. On the Motor Home, this note: "Payne: I'm at the Havana Hotel. Room 333. Get a move on. C. J. Clovis, Savonarola Batworks, Inc."

Clovis himself looked petulantly from the window of Room 333 with no certainty that Payne would ever come. He could see the reflecting metal roofs of Key West, the vegetation growing up between and, across town, the Coast Guard and Standard Oil docks. He wanted to play tennis but he only had one arm and one leg.

He tried to interest himself in the builder's plans for the tower which was to be built on nearby Mente Chica Key. But he was upset. He wanted vodka. He wanted a tart. That girl of Payne's was a tart. Why didn't he get rid of her? A rich tart with an old rich tart for a mother and a successful stupid male tart for a father. He should have hit the bastards for a fifteen-level bat atrium.

Clovis was quite upset. He had an ailment.

In a small glowing plastic cube hovered the numeral 3. Payne pressed the cube with his index finger and the doors slid shut and the two of them soared upwards. Presently, they stopped and the doors opened and there was a sign.

←300–350

351–399→

Payne turned left down the corridor, leading Ann by the hand. Ann's prole mania made her strike up conversations with every Cuban chambermaid that were singularly brittle in the vastitude of their misunderstanding.

Finally, room 333. A knock.

"Yes?"

"It's me."

"Come in. I can't come to the door. I've got an ailment."

They went in. Clovis was on the bed, the covers pulled up under his chin. He looked peaked.

"I've got one this time," he said in the chanting voice he always used in speaking of illness.

"What."

"I've got a real dandy on this run," he said.

"The other leg."

"No." Clovis looked out of the window a long time. A tear tracked down his cheek. He did not look back at them. "My heart is on the fritz."

They sat down. This was a sorry way to start the venture. There was work to be done. It was warm. You could go for a swim and all be friends.

"From a fugitive's point of view," said Clovis, pulling himself together, "this is the worst place in the world. You can't get off the highway anywhere from here back to the mainland for a hundred-and-fifty miles. The bastards would have you funneled."

"Are you planning to be a fugitive?"

"No. Payne, how are your hemorrhoids?"

"Fine; thank you for asking."

"Take care of them before they get out of hand. Once they're thrombosed you get impaction and every other damn thing."

"They're already thrombosed."

"Then you're in for a postoperative Waterloo."

"No, I'm not. I'm not having them operated on."

"Well, that's just what I wanted to ask you."

"Ask me what?"

"Whether you wouldn't join me in the hospital."

"No, I won't."

"This time I'm scared."

"I don't care. The answer is no."

"Where is your humanity?" Ann inquired, thinking of how that lay at the roots of Western culture.

"Among the dying grunions," Payne replied, "at Redondo Beach."

They put everything—Hudson Hornet, wagon and motor home—under a shade tree behind the Two Friends Bar. Payne fed the bats and wondered if they missed their home in the limestone cave. It had gotten hot.

Once inside the motor home, Payne drew all the blinds and turned on the air conditioner. It was soon comfortable and they napped on the broad foam bed. When they awoke, it was dark. Ann was chewing a large wad of gum and sipping from a bottle of whiskey she had bought at the Two Friends Bar while Payne slept. She poured him a drink without saying anything. She was strolling around without her clothes on.

Payne swung his legs over the side of the bed. He looked and felt exhausted. Ann pivoted around toward him, the Nikon to her eye, and photographed him.

It didn't take her long to find the radio. She turned on a Cuban station with its Sten-gun dance music and began to pachanga up and down the aisle in some inexplicable transport. "Dance?" she called to Payne. He declined. The music was discouragingly loud. He could hardly keep his eye on her as she caromed around the inside of the motor home. Once when she shot by he made a grab for her. She kept streaking around, breasts lunging. "Dance?" she cried again. He refused, watching in wonder, and undressed, folding his clothes. "Wallflower!" He thought this painstaking reserve would be good for things. But he had an erection; so he wasn't fooling anyone. It was aimed at his own forehead; and he felt a giddiness as of danger. He suddenly believed that the engorged penis acquires all its blood from the brain. He made Ann come over and sit on it; and she got violently exercised by the procedure. At the supreme time, his whole head seemed to be opaque. "Egad," he barked shortly. Payne really looked at her for the first time that night; she seemed awfully big and the cascade of silver hair disoriented him entirely. When he withdrew, a translucent tendril connected them an instant longer, then fell glistening on one of her perfect thighs.

Payne turned off Radio Havana. Someone was giving the sugar quotas, province by province, *arroba* by *arroba*. He found a brownie with walnuts and ate it, not bothering to dress. He had a little drink. He looked around himself.

173

Ann was lying on the couch next to the settee. Overhead a lighting that felt sourceless but was probably fluorescent shone with a lunar absence of shadows. It was like being in an atomic submarine; perhaps, inside a vacuum cleaner was more accurate. Everything was built in. Nothing stood clear of the curved walls. The whole inside of the motor home was a variation on the tube theme. They were in an intestine, Payne thought giddily; and digestion was worse than anything the Waring Blender could do to you.

Payne thought that the rug had been pulled out from under his crazy act. Ann's was beginning to look a little more marginal than his, if that was possible. Yet he had—he thought—a purpose behind his and still did; which was, in the vernacular, getting it all together. On the old motorcycle excursion, he had tried to draw a line around it all; now he was trying to color it all in.

From time to time that night, drunken shrimpers beat on the door. "Invasion of privacy," thought Payne. He had nowhere else to put the vehicles; so this activity would have to be discouraged completely. They tried to sleep awhile; but it was never long before the uproar began anew. Then he heard a number of them arguing in some drunk's comedy and one of them tried to force open the door. "Breaking and entering," Payne thought. They knew there was a female in here and had gone entirely doggy. The door of the motor home bulged and Ann was frightened completely if temporarily out of her hillbilly act. Payne got up, rifling through drawers.

He found in Clovis' underwear drawer the revolver he had recently employed to bushwhack the tires on his Hudson Hornet. Payne was wearing only his shorts. Nevertheless, when he opened the door, stepped down and circulated among the drunks with the revolver, he was found to be, in his own way, strangely impressive. The drunks had a leader in the person of a stringy individual with a Confederate flag tattooed on his forearm that said, *Hell, no, I ain't forgetting.* This man proposed to disarm Payne and go aboard. He said that anyone who pulled a gun better be prepared to use it. But when Payne took a handful of his cheek, put the barrel of the gun inside of his mouth and offered to blow his brains all over the Gulf of Mexico, there was a loss of interest in tampering with the motor home or going aboard at all. They could tell that Payne had reached that curious emotional plateau which did not necessarily have anything to do with anger that, once gained, let one man kill another. Payne would never have known until he had done it; but complete strangers could tell beforehand. So Payne went back aboard only wondering why he had not been nervous; and not realizing how near he had been to a most significant human act; while the drunks now squealing, revving, popping clutches and roaring off were all somewhat sobered up with how close it had been.

The owner of the bar came out. "Sorry those old boys took it in their heads to pester you. Sorry as hell."

"No bother at all," Payne said. The man was studying him, trying to guess how much he would put up with. "I do feel you ought to know that the next time it happens I will kill people." Payne thought he was telling a lie. The owner's face whitened.

"I'll pass that on," he said.

"In the end they'll like it that way better."

The bar owner laughed very slightly.

"I expect they will," he agreed. "I will sholy pass it on."

Payne climbed back in and locked the door. Ann looked at him as he put the pistol up. She had photographed him

175

standing in the doorway in his shorts, as he turned back into the artificial light, the revolver hanging by its trigger guard from his forefinger. He looked transported.

"I'm a king bee, baby," he said.

"Have you fed the bats?" she asked.

First thing in the morning, Payne and Clovis met with a Cuban named Diego Fama who would act as co-foreman and interpreter on the tower project. Clovis wanted to use entirely refugee labor. He said he wanted to do his part to make opposition to Castro attractive.

Diego Fama was a muscular contractor type, his Cuban–Indian physiognomy to the contrary notwithstanding. He had startling big forearms which he crisscrossed high on his chest when listening. He did not speak English particularly well; but listened to the planning with heavy, Germanic attention. He already understood the project better than Payne and Clovis. "Easy job," he said precisely when the talk was done.

"How long?"

"Under a week." The news embarrassed both Payne and Clovis with respect to the price they were getting; but not for long.

"How many men?"

"I figure that out," Diego Fama said. "I say now though possibly twenty of these persons."

"Where will you find them?" Payne asked.

"I figure that out," Fama replied balefully.

"And what is your subcontracting charge?"

"Three thousand dollars," Fama said. It was unbelievably cheap.

"That's high," Clovis said, "but we accept. When do we start?"

"Monday in the morning."

When Fama was gone, Clovis wrote out a bill on the kind of pad waitresses carry and gave it to Payne for examination.

BILL

1 Bat Tower	$16,000.00
1500 Standard Bats	$1500.00
1 Guano Trap w/ storage receptacle	$1000.00
1 Special Epoxy Tropical Paint, Brushes and Thinner	$500.00

THANK YOU. PLEASE CALL AGAIN.

"I'm surprised at you," said Ann back at the motor home, "treating the old fart like that."

"Are you?"

"He's scared to death his ailment is going to carry him off."

"How would it help if I went in and had my butt trimmed?"

"Surprised at you," she said, "leaving him in the lurch."

"I'm not leaving him in the lurch."

"The lurch."

"I'm not."

"Explain it if you're not," she said and as he started to rage, she raised her camera to photograph him. He got in a conventional wedding-portrait smile before she could snap it. "Surprised at you," she said.

"I'll visit him every day," Payne said.

Ann had been out photographing trash, gas stations and Dairy Queens. "Leaving him in the lurch." She turned the turretlike lens of the Nikon Photomic FTN and fired point-blank. "You look so wiped out I wanted to get it on film with all this plastic crap around you. It's too much."

"I hope it comes out," said Payne.

"I got one of you last night that was priceless. You were making a drink in your underwear and I must say you were sagging from end to end."

"I'll want to see that one."

"You will."

"Tell me this, are you having a little social experiment here? Is this what was once called 'slumming it'?"

"I don't know what you mean."

"You tell me what it is then," said Payne.

"It's art."

"Well," Payne said, "any more fucking art around here and I'm going to commence something unfortunate. I had enough art at the hands of the Mum and Dad."

"I cannot understand you," Ann said; but she had got a glimpse of what the shrimpers had seen and she knew it was going to be necessary to shut up.

"I can't understand you," she said at a distance.

"Persevere."

Ann left the motor home and skulked around the back of the bar. Payne watched her making desultory photographs of citrus rinds and inorganic refuse. A fat and drunken tourist in bermudas went by and she followed him for awhile, snapping away at his behind, and then returned to the motor home.

She had every hope that her dark night of the soul would be on film.

In the middle of the night, Payne suddenly awoke with a terrible, unspecific feeling of sadness. He waited until he

178

had a grip on himself. Then, he woke Ann. "You're right," he said.

"About what."

"About Clovis. I'll go to the hospital with him."

Ann kissed him. "You're always thinking of others," she said.

"Will you feed the bats?"

17

Payne called Clovis and told him. He could feel his relief over the wire. "I don't want to go it alone this time." Payne felt as if confirmed in his decision; though he was himself frightened by the operation in store for him.

Construction of the tower was going to be in the hands of Diego Fama.

The hospital arrangements were wangled artfully by Clovis who alluded to his own medical history in veiled tones. It sounded gothic and exciting. The personnel were thrilled by Clovis' lack of limbs. He seemed the real thing in a hospital dogged with health and minor problems.

A not unoccupied elevator passed through the building; it carried a solitary patient in gold embossed plastic bedroom slippers and an uncomfortable shift tied around his mottled neck. His hair was de rigueur wino, combed back and close. At the top floor, the door opened and he ran for daylight, radiant with his own brand of hyperesthesia.

After the proctological examination, during which Payne's surgical need was specified as "acute," Payne fell

180

asleep. He had been horrified by the doctor's steering that machine through his inwards like the periscope of a U-boat.

The Monroe County Hospital was an unusual place. Situated next to a dump ("Sanitary land fill"), the smoke of burning garbage blew through the wards. Meanwhile, Clovis was wheeled around to all the testing facilities. He had a cardiogram, an electroencephalogram, an X-ray. His urine, stool and blood were tested. They took skin scrapings and hair samples. They weighed C. J. Clovis.

The curtain was drawn between the two beds. Payne could hear the doctor and Clovis talking. The doctor demanded to know exactly what the complaint was.

"My body's all aching and racked with pain," said Clovis.

The doctor, a feisty former fighter pilot of the United States Navy said simply, "There isn't anything the matter with you. You are in the habit of illness. You ought to get out."

"What is your name?"

"Doctor Proctor."

"I'll have your ass."

"I've arranged," said Proctor plainly, "to have you put out. You are in the habit of illness."

The doctor passed the screen where Payne lay. There was silence when he was gone. In a while, Clovis hobbled around to the foot of Payne's bed.

"You heard that?"

"Yes—"

"I'll have his ass."

By that evening, Clovis was gone. By the next morning he was back. He had no doctor assigned to him at all. Since there were plenty of beds, they agreed to let nurses run tests on him from time to time and to use him as a kind of training doll. Clovis slept all the time. He was having a holiday. It was rather boring for Payne and bad times were ruining his posture. He walked around in a curve. He looked like a genius.

They never got a girl as pretty as Ann in here. A good number of the women who had come knew what they were getting into and opted for it out of some carnal compulsion. Which is to say that a certain number of gang-bangs had originated here; and were remembered. Nevertheless, she held her own at the bar, elbow to elbow with the shrimpers in their khaki clothes and their ineffable odeur of the docks.

When a fight broke out later over who exactly was going to talk to her and in what sequence, she saw the whole bloody mess as an Ektachrome fantasia hanging on the walls of the Guggenheim.

Standing next to the pool table, waiting for his shot and never having glanced up at the fight at all, was a shrimper in his late thirties who looked like a slightly handsomer, slightly more fleshed-out version of Hank Williams or any number of other hillbilly singers, save that he wore khaki fisherman's clothes. He spoiled an easy bank shot and said, "Them cushions is soft. Don't nobody replace nothin here?"

He walked straight over to where Ann stood. "This is no place for a lady," he said. "Have you ever been to Galveston by sea?"

All the next day, Payne and Clovis spent on the telephone. They had decided to let Diego Fama and family go ahead and build the tower. There were many questions of credit to be settled, equipment and ready-mix concrete to

182

be secured. The tensest conversations—and they were Payne's—were with the officers of the Mid-Keys Boosters who had been sold on the thing in the first place by Clovis. They were testy to begin with and grew more so the more money was required of them.

Payne tried to reach Ann at the Two Friends Bar and got unsatisfactory answers.

Diego Fama's mother called and wanted to know what to feed the bats.

Flat on his back, Payne had a chance to fret about Ann. She was going haywire. But he thought he could help her over the phase if he could be with her. His hemorrhoids had seemed to come between them. It seemed hideously unnecessary. What had people done in ages gone by about such a condition? Nothing. And their lives had transpired like a stately pas de deux amid plentiful antiques and objets d'art of real interest to the connoisseur. We each of us know instinctively that hemorrhoids were unknown before our century. It is the pressure of the times, symbolically expressed. Their removal is mere cosmetic surgery.

When he browsed in the hallways it had seemed that the sickrooms full of, in some cases, the most monstrously injured or ailing creatures, should give onto trees, lawns and ruminant cars driven, now and then, by people with nothing in the slightest the matter with them. Nothing.

He pretended that he was among the dying and made himself quite sad with the exercise. The doctor enters. I'm sorry to have to tell you this but all of us sometime. I'm afraid it's. I know, doctor, I know. And the others. Is it known among the others. That I'm to. And the little girls. Will they or would they take in hand the shy item of a man who will not be here?

183

From his window, which was none too clean, he saw many a scalped tree and sorry palm on an expanse of asphalt. God knows how, but they say you make friends here. Who never forget you. Payne looked around him. My Christ, they'll drive their expensive steel in my fanny. And at the end I am to pick up the tab. There you are, doctor. All those simoleons for what you have done to me.

Beside Payne, asleep, a certain misshapen person, an object of great curiosity: Clovis. He had made a mess of his bed. Payne—still starched and ventilated in his back-buttoned shift—noticed that. Rumple sheets enough and they appeared to turn yellow. Possibly it was the abysmal light that threw so many soft, upsetting shadows. Payne felt his face had elongated. He knew his voice would not be strong.

But Clovis slept on, his face running all over an immense forearm. He lay on his stomach and pushed forward with his leg, sleeping like a baby.

"Close your mouth on the therm." Payne could taste the alcohol. The nurse had that flush, clean prettiness that might have been blown from a single bead of thermodynamic plastic; that beauty so illusively distributed among majorettes and Breck shampoo girls that certain Rotarian interests have attempted to isolate as a national type.

Thinking of what was to come, pain appeared to him in a number of guises, the main one being something minute, an itching follicle, that expanded like a sonofabitch. Why me?

The next time the pretty nurse came, she drew Payne's curtain around him, thus cutting off some incipient conversational gloating between Payne and Clovis on the subject of the bat tower.

The girl plainly came to her profession via the misrepresentations of Nancy Drew. Fluffing pillows. There, doesn't that feel just a lot better now? Roll over. She used his entire can to drive a column of mercury. He wondered why she took his temperature there, when she hadn't before. She was building to something.

He rested his head, wan. Around the top of the curtain, a white painted pipe bisected the ceiling. He could hear Clovis next to him fold a newspaper roughly; its shadow jerked on the ceiling.

The nurse laid out her instruments on the cloth-covered tray beside him: the thermometer, some sort of shaving materials, and a dire rubberoid article with chambers, petcocks and tubes. Payne ran scared.

On his stomach, his neck cricked upward uncomfortably, he took a fix on the wall and waited in silence for the first touch. In an endless instant, he felt her tentative fingers plucking unsuccessfully at the edge of the shift, cold fingertips grazing his affrighted bottom, then up went the shift and Payne felt the horror of circulating air. He heard the sigh of some escaping pressure, smelled soapy menthol and felt a billow of soft cream smoothed onto his perineum and backside by the peerless hand of the young nurse. Perspiration poured from his face into the absorbent pillowcase.

At the first scraping, which was simultaneous with the first involuntary little noise from the nurse, he turned over his shoulder and looked. He saw her inclined face behind a broad, heart-shaped silhouette; tears streamed down as she manipulated the razor, rinsing it when it overloaded with shaving cream in a bowl on her tray. This was an episode that appeared in no edition of Nancy Drew stories.

Her cheeks were withdrawn and her face was an altogether imploring image of loss, grief, unitemized sorrow and what not. Finally, she gave his glossy stern a wipe of towel and Payne raked down the shift. She pushed his hand away and choked, "No."

She broke out the rubber heart, swollen with liquid, and buried its nozzle in his fanny. Holding the heavy, swollen bag in both hands, she seemed to proffer it. Payne imagined the unsightly article to contain ice water. He was impaled on a frozen stalagmite and gritted down hard until she withdrew the nozzle. He looked back to see her tears but found instead that she was laughing silently. It was disturbing.

That would have been otherwise a moment for clear and immediate thought. He would have liked to see what happened to a gesture of friendship with the nurse toward who knew what. As it was, though, his feet made a furious, impatient squeaking on the waxed institutional floor. He ran through a couple of complicated maneuvers—ones that would have been illegal in an automobile: reckless U-turns, especially—just to get around the tables to the bathroom where, sitting, he had an utter cathartic letting-go as though chambers, membranes, tiny bulkheads and walls all collapsed at once in a single directional rush.

When he was finished, that careful, Byronic grandiosity that he was inclined to cultivate was completely gone. And he felt, still sitting, like a simple shriveled fly.

"How long have I been asleep?" Clovis asked.
"A long time. I don't know."
"How did I act? Did I say anything."
"You just lay there and twitched like a dog."

It wasn't long after dinner that the nurse came again. She drew Payne's curtain, herself inside, and gave him enough of her unnerving smile-play that he began to fancy trying something. Throwing up his shift behind she whispered in his ear, "You foul your linen, mister, and you're in Dutch with me!" Payne, thrilled, not hearing the words at all, not more anyway than the airy voice and smelling her fabulous dimestore jasmine, tried to twist around and kiss her.

But she deftly thrust a lubricated nozzle into his rectum, really deflating him, and delivered a column of fluid thirteen feet in length, though certainly not as the crow flies.

A moment later, catching Clovis' eyes, he cleared out, his feet squealing like wharf rats on the hard floor. This time, his easement of himself was a progressive collapse of his intestines behind their emptying contents.

From the room, he heard Clovis laughing, "Mae West! Man overboard! What are you thinking about in there?"

"Bombs."

"Bombs!" Clovis said with alarm. *"What bombs?"*

Then, after the third enema, he didn't have to void himself. He couldn't figure it out. Nothing happened. After twenty minutes of studying Payne, Clovis said, "You go yet?"

"No."

"What's keeping you?"

"I don't have to go anymore," Payne said with irritation.

"You didn't go after a high colonic?"

"I don't have to. Is that okay?"

"Jesus, that is something else again. Not take one after a high colonic. Not after he had one. That really takes it."

Five minutes of silence.

"Want to have a whirlpool bath?" Clovis asked. Payne focused on him.

Payne followed Jack Clovis into a large room. Clovis leaned his crutches up and hobbled and hopped along the high fluorescent-lit walls. The room was a uniform, clean, prison gray and a gutter ran in the concrete around the base of its walls. In the center of the room was a circular drain that held a metal insert like the piece that is on the burner of a gas stove.

In this room were half a dozen identical stainless-steel whirlpool baths. Deferring to possibility, Clovis adjusted the one nearest the door for Payne. They had already located the john in a military way. The bath was now filled with surging water. Payne reached in and felt the agreeable temperature throbbing powerfully against his hand. Clovis went to fill his own a few feet away. Payne got in with an inrush of breath. He felt the maniacal sensuality of the tropical water ply his flesh, reduce him to speechlessness. Clovis climbed into his, holding on, white-knuckled, with the one hand. Payne sank into seizing warmth until only his head remained above the agitated surface.

His brain sagged gently into a peaceful and celestial neutrality. His eyes moistened from the lacy steam that arose from the water as though from a druid's tarn. His mind was little more than the cipher which activates the amoeba and the paramecium.

Only then did the labyrinth of his system begin to confound him; first with bowel misgivings which, in his beatitude, he tried to ignore; then with a series of seizures that ran through his viscera like lightning. It was too late to ignore them.

He grabbed the stainless-steel sides as though it were a

tossing boat and, moaning aloud, felt the sharp contractions of that most privy and yet imperious of the intestines.

Looking down in his abandonment of all hope, he saw, as though a cloud had crossed the sun, the water darken suddenly around him. And he knew that the worst had happened.

He wrenched at the controls violently until the bath shut off and he sat in the now stilled fluid. A moment later, Clovis, sensing something, carefully shut off his own and the two men sat with new silence roaring up around them.

Suddenly, Jack Clovis wrinkled his face violently.

"Good Christ, Payne! What in God's name are you cooking there!"

Payne got to his feet looking, really, as though he had just come from Miami, a city he never liked that much. And he was too far gone to be amused.

18

Doctor Proctor, manipulant-grandee of the proctoscope, an instrument which brings to the human eye vistas which are possibly forbidden (possibly not), lazed at home watching the Olympic bobsled trials on ABC's Wide World of Sports. The lush blue carpet cuddled his pink physician's heels and when he walked across its Middle Eastern richesse, he pretended to himself that it was the guts, tripe and visceral uproar amid which his profession obliged him to live.

Here it was different. Here where the goggle-eyed street urchins of his most valuable canvases stared at one another from the soft contours of his walls, he was inclined to dream of all the things he no longer was. Then, he would find himself a little droopy and all too inclined to pop a couple of amphetamines from his big fat doctor's stash. And then, when he overdid, as he did tonight, he would be the energetic boy of before, laughing, crying and gouging quickly at his crotch in that little athlete's gesture of look what we have here.

Tonight, snuffling a trifle with the upshot of his high,

Proctor made his way to the darkling trophy room of his Key West home; and, once again, commenced vacuuming the hundreds of dim upright mouths of his trophies with his well-used Hoover. Standing waist-deep among the winged victories and gaping loving cups, he knew, somehow, who he was.

Often, in such a mood, his nurse would appear to his imagination, often up to something freakish which Proctor could not ordinarily have contrived. Recurrently, on the other hand, she would appear nude and aslither atop an immense conduit covered with non-fat vegetable shortening. Such a thought could not have been foreborne without eventual relief; and his little wrist-flicks at himself came to linger for the serious business at hand.

But nothing disruptive, all in all. Proctor functioned. So it was that in the morning hours when most people were asleep, Proctor, who never *had* slept, headed for the clinic in his green Aston Martin DB-4. Heel-and-toeing to keep his revs up, he brodied and drifted through the damp morning streets of the Island City.

Well, he said to himself, life is a shakedown cruise. Wanna bet? Through housework, pills and orgasms, he had lost eight pounds since nightfall. He hadn't been on a zombie run like this since the service where, with his usual athletic finesse, he had distinguished himself as a fighter pilot.

He had flown the almost legendary and sinister fireship, the carrier-based F4 Phantom, making night runs and day runs with the same penetrating fanaticism that vanished with very little aging and required the bolstering of pills.

For a while, all the pilot's bugaboos had haunted him: night landings on a heaving carrier deck in the fierce rocket-laden thirty-eight-thousand-pound flying piano, hoping to hell that on that blackened deck the aircraft would find one of the four arrester wires and keep him from deep-sixing off the bow.

Vertigo: One cloudless night on the South China Sea, Proctor had been practicing his sidewinder runs and barrel rolls and high-performance climbs with the afterburner pouring the last possible thrust beyond Mach II; when suddenly his brain would no longer equilibrate and he couldn't tell which end was up; somehow he flew pure instrument on the carrier landing, straight on for the Fresnel light on the ship's stern, catching the fourth wire and snatching up short of a hundred-and-eighty-degree view of the blackened South China Sea. He felt the entire rotation of his brain; all the physical perceptions which were his only moral facts gently rocked into place again; and the next day he started cinching them down with goof-balls.

Soon enough, the younger pilots who had begun to resent his sheepish hand on the stick saw the old fiend was intact after all; and from then on, when he came in from a strike with leftover fuel, he sneaked in around the islands and blew up junks and sank native craft with his shock wave and really made himself felt.

Naturally, the skipper who had been watching this appealing Yankee Doodle and who was alerted to this new panache by the revived Proctor habit of picking his arrester wire on landings—traditional fighter-jock's machismo caper—called him in and, chuckling, told him to lay off because the gooks were going to load the junks with anti-aircraft equipment and start weeding out those four-million-dollar Phantoms.

Proctor quipped that he didn't care if they got the plane as long as the seat worked. But the old skipper reminded him that Charlie would find you if you ejected and make a Countess Mara with your tongue. And still Proctor didn't give a damn, really didn't give a damn! He boomed, bombed, blasted and killed and sank small craft the same as always except now he did it during bombing halts when he was supposed to have been on reconnaissance.

Into his continuous vile blue yonder, Yankee Doodle Proctor went, high as high could be on various purloinings from the flight surgeon's old kit bag; still masturbatory as all get out, he sometimes gouged at the crotch of his flight suit in the middle of combat, giggled when flak gently rocked the aircraft or snuffed one of the smaller Skyhawks that always went on strike with the dreamy, invulnerable McDonnell Phantoms.

Sometimes, in over the trees supersonically, he would get glimpses of Migs deployed on jungle runways, some of them scrambling. And once a SAM ground-to-air missile, like a white enamel tree trunk, appeared in the formation and Proctor purposely let it pick him up and follow for a thousand feet before he duped its computer brain into overshooting. Again, he giggled and gouged at his flight suit to imagine that prize gook investment on its pitiful try at killing the sun, which Proctor had substituted for himself by way of a crazy parabolic maneuver that made the pale metal wings of the Phantom lift gently with the force of God knew how many G's; that made even old giggling Yankee Doodle's face pull and flow toward his ass; that made the smooth voluptuous curves of Asia, caressed by his shock wave, clog with unimaginable scrollery of trees and detail. He climbed, sonic booms volleying over the country, after-burners pulled to the utmost and cleared out at fifty thousand feet in whorls, volutes, beautiful spirals of vapor.

Three weeks of gouging had made a shiny spot on his flight suit.

How close this all now seemed. And, really, it spoiled

his driving; a sports car for God's sake with its stupid bland instruments that indicated the ridiculous landbound progress of the machine. By the time he was in the staff parking lot, he was cranky. A pharmaceutical supply truck was parked at the loading bay and Proctor, already coming down, imagined eating his way through the truck, stem to stern. Inside the first door, he spotted a gabble of creepy little interns with careful telltale stethoscopes hanging out of their pockets. Proctor told them to break it up and they did. They knew Proctor would besmirch them at staff meetings. In the involuted parlance of the world of interns, Proctor was an "asshole." But this was unfair to Proctor, an altogether harmlessly overpaid popinjay of the medical profession.

"On the table."

Payne obeyed. He could see the doctor was not in the mood for chatter. Neither, for that matter, was he. Endless nightmares of the possible violations of his body had left him rather testy.

"How do you mean, doctor?"

"I mean on the table. Right now. Crossways."

The nurse came in and the doctor looked up. Payne sat across the examining table.

"Where are we with this guy?" the doctor asked. The nurse looked at her board.

"He had the pentobarbital sodium at six this morning. Then the atropine and morphine an hour ago. I—"

"How do you feel?" the doctor asked Payne.

"Okay."

"Relaxed and ready for the operation?"

"Vaguely." Proctor looked him over, thought: tough guy with the lightest possible glazing of civilization: two years at the outside in some land-grant diploma mill. "I forget," the doctor went on to his nurse, "are these external?"

"A little of both."

"Ah, so. And thrombosed were they not?"

"I should say."

A wispy man, the dread anesthesiologist, came in wheeling a sort of portable autoclave with his ghastly instruments inside. Through the drugs he had been given that morning, Payne could feel some slow dread arise. As for Proctor, this skillful little creep—Reeves by name—with his hair parted low over his left ear and carefully deployed over his bald head, was an object of interest and admiration. He watched him lay out the materials with some delight and waited for the little man's eagerness to crest at the last possible moment before saying, "Thank you, Reeves. I think I'd rather." Reeves darkened and left the room. "Hunch your shoulders, Mister—"

"Payne. Like that?"

"Farther. There you go."

After his little moment with Reeves, Proctor had second thoughts. He knew the sacral block shouldn't be taken casually; and he didn't do them often enough to be really in practice. But what the hell. This guy was preoperatively well prepared; he'd just wind it up.

"Nurse, what kind of lumbar puncture needle did Reeves bring us?"

"A number twenty-two, doctor."

Proctor chuckled. That Reeves was a real mannerist. A little skinny needle like that; but maybe that's how they were doing it now. Used to be you had a needle like a rifle barrel and you'd get cerebrospinal fluid running down the clown's back. It made for a fast job but memorable headaches for the patient afterwards.

Proctor went at it. He pressed the needle into the fourth lumbar interspace well into the subarachnoid region and withdrew two cc's of spinal fluid which he mixed with a hundred mg's of novocaine crystals in a hyperbaric solution which he reinjected confident he had Payne's ass dead to the world for four good hours.

Just for precaution—it was really Reeves's precaution— he gave Payne fifty mg's of ephedrine sulfate in the arm. "Keep this man sitting up straight," Proctor said and went outside to the drinking fountain and popped another goofball, this one covered with lint from his pocket. He peered sadly into the middle distance and thought: *I was the darling of the fleet.*

Payne was wheeled by, on his way to the operating room. He began to review his life. Very little of it would come. He could go back—lying there numbed, the victim of purloined spinal fluid—about two weeks with any solidity; then, flashes. As: boarding school, Saturday morning, in a spectral study hall for unsatisfactory students; Payne and three other dunces watched over like meat by the master on duty, in pure Spring light, in silence. At one window of the hall, striped boy athletes rock noiselessly past for batting practice; a machine pitched hardballs out of a galvanized hopper and the base paths were still muddy. Payne shielding his eyes in apparent concentration, occasionally dozes, occasionally slips a magazine out from under the U. S. History text: *Guns And Ammo.* In his mind, he cradles a Finnish Sako rifle, sits on a ridge in the Canadian Rockies that glitters with mica and waits two hundred years for a Big Horn Ram. Something moves a few yards up the draw: The master on duty has spotted *Guns And Ammo.* Payne's heart whirls in his chest and loses traction.

"Miss?" Payne asks.

"Sir?"

"I feel like a dead Egyptian. You and Proctor are fixing to pull my brain out of my nose."

"No, sir!"

"I feel that life has handed me one in the snot locker. You see I'm the last buffalo. And I'm dying of a sucking chest wound. Isn't there something you could do in a case like mine? Some final ecstasy you could whip up?"

"Nothing that comes to mind, sir."

"Miss, if my beak falls open and cries are heard during Doctor Proctor's knifework, will that be it, as far as you're concerned? I mean, will you sign off on yours truly? As another has?"

"Possibly a leetle."

"In other circumstances I would be a simple hero to you. But maybe your life already is not unencumbered. Is there a certain someone?"

Proctor strode in. "Let's do it." Payne intoned a helpless sphincteric dirge. He was in terror. This room was filled with strange and frightful machinery which would have been the envy of any number of pirates whose names are household words.

"Will there be pain?" Payne inquired.

"I don't know what you mean."

"Surely the word rings one little bell in your medical carillon tower." Payne regretted his words instantly. He did not want to antagonize Proctor.

"It appears," said the doctor to the nurse, "that the medication has taken our friend by storm."

Proctor looked down from his end of the operating table. He had Payne on his back, in the lithotomy position; not the one Proctor was most comfortable with; but the only one a serious proctologist would consider with spinal

197

anesthesia via the hyperbaric solutions that Reeves found so irresistible. Reeves! What a bleary little cornball.

From this perspective, Proctor saw with a tiny almost atavistic horror the ring of thrombosed hemorrhoids. And it was now a question of demonstrating the internal complications so that they could be excised without any further fiddling around.

Proctor thought helplessly of how he could have been a big, clean career aviator instead of staring up some wise guy's dirt chute.

He inserted his index finger well into Payne's rectum withdrawing and reinserting several times without, in his opinion, sufficiently extruding the internal hemorrhoids. In a moment of impatience and almost pique, he stuffed Payne's rectum with wads of dry gauze which he hauled out slowly dragging the hemorrhoids with them. Now he had a perfectly beastly little mess to clean up. The entire anal verge was clustered with indisputably pathological extrusions. Proctor sighed languorously.

With a certain annoyance, he dilated Payne's sphincter to an anal aperture of two centimeters and then, making more work space for himself, rather zealously went for, and got, three centimeters without tearing even a teensy bit of sphincteric muscle. He swiftly clipped four forceps into position to keep the site exposed. A smile broke out on his face as he remembered his Asian days.

All of the sound and movements around Payne were informed with the most sinister lack of ordinary reality. Implements passed his vision which were not unlike those with which we eat; yet, somehow, something was wrong with them. They had crooked handles or the ones you thought were spoons had trap doors or when they touched each other they rang with an unearthly clarity. And surrounding the hard if intolerable precision of all this weaponry were various loose bags, drooping neoprene tubes, cups of deep blubbery gels, fleecy, inorganic sponges in space-age colors, and the masked, make-up lacking face of the nurse, her hair yanked back in utilitarian severity.

Around himself, he could hear the doctor talking, nipping off the words as if to challenge a misunderstanding of his grandiose medical technicalities. Payne felt that something like the same smugness and expertise must attend the performance of electrocutions, the kind of officiousness that would make a condemned man hesitate before using the terms "hot seat" or "fry."

Proctor was cranky. He needn't have made this kind of a mess. And so he muttered with the usual authoritarian voice that there wasn't one thing there he couldn't clean up. Not one.

Still, he didn't know what had become of his coordination. Ordinarily, he could incise the most perfect demi-eclipse around the base of the hemorrhoid and dissect the varix from the external sphincter with a deft turn of the wrist. Truly, this was surgery that could have been performed with a rotary mower; and yet, he was barely up to it.

So, instead of a nice clean finish, he had to hunt up and down the patient's dirt chute for bleed points, stop them—in one case resorting to catgut, so nasty was the lesion—and then impatiently make a thick dressing the size of a catcher's mitt to sop up the serosanguineous ooze that was surely going to be a part of this man's postoperative period.

He had Payne wheeled away unconscious after a veritable hosing down with demerol. He indicated he would have the nurse remain. When the door was shut and Proctor looked around at the spattered operating room, the nurse stood without motion. Proctor spotted smart wads of disapprobation in her eyes.

"Nice little rectum you left him with there," she said in a brave squeak, "with your cut-and-try surgery there."

"A bleeder."

"That poor boy," she said. "I have never in my life witnessed a thing like that. It almost looked like you were trying to make some sort of meal back there."

"What meal!"

"I don't know, some, I don't know, almost like some sort of pasta fazoula or—"

"Pasta fazoula! Are you Italian? Pasta fazoula is this great Italian dish—" The nurse waved him silent with a harsh and impatient motion.

"God, Doctor, I was illustrating something oh never mind I . . ."

"Nurse, I used to sit on the starboard catapult during international emergencies, waiting to go bomb. In a forty-thousand-pound aircraft with wings that wouldn't glide a sparrow if the engines ever failed: a flying piano. And me in the driver's seat getting to feel more and more like pure crash-cargo, lady. And from my viewpoint on the steam catapult I could see, below me in the waters of the South China Sea, twenty-foot man-eating sharks that had been feeding on Oriental sea burials for a thousand years. How do you think I felt?"

"How?"

"Punk. Those sharks would break up a funeral halfway through the services and there's me on the starboard catapult: one flame-out and you're so much fish food. And you tell me pasta fazoula."

"But Doctor I—"

"Tell me cut-and-try, do you?"

"Doctor, I—"

"I've had enough. I thought that after war a man could return to a life of service with interludes of silence spent among a tasteful collection of art objects."

"Doctor, how can I make it up to you?"

Payne lay quiet as a fossil in the deep sweeping benignity of demerol, the Kuda Bux of Key West. Pale surgical lights rolled by as moons. Then it was blistering dry and hot; an expanse of macadam curled at the far edges and made twenty-nine identical mountains. Payne held a big, ice cold chronometer.

A bedside view would have shown that, if only for the time being, Proctor, Ann and Clovis had made of Nicholas Payne pure meat.

Finally, in the middle of the night, he woke up laughing in complete weakness. "*Seep, seep, seep.*" Clovis, in perfect health, yelled, "Shut up, can't you! I'm a dead goose as it is for crying out loud."

Payne opened his mind like the sweet dusty comic strip from a pink billet of Fleer's bubblegum and saw things as deep and appropriate as soft nudes on the noses of B29's. He saw longhorn cattle being driven over the Golden Gate Bridge, St. Teresa of Avila at the Mocambo, pale blue policemen nose-to-bung in an azure nimbus around the moon.

He had happy dreams. He could hear the punctual ringing of the first pair of steel taps on his first pair of blue suede shoes and remembered Jerry Lee Lewis climbing a piano in Miami in fiery lemon-colored underwear, assaulting the keys with hands feet head knees, two-foot platinum hair flapping the Steinway contours and howling *GREAT BOWLS OF FAR!*

Jerry Lee knew how to treat a piano.

. .

He awoke early in the morning in the sharpest kind of pain and with a feeling of clarity. The principal menaces were behind. And the rather murky situation with Ann seemed to have fallen into place; though he would have been hard put to say where. He felt as if he were collecting into one shape and that he would soon make a kind of sudden expansion. He would stop feeling the little nerve headaches urge their way up from his neocortex. He would get his saliva back and his lips wouldn't stick to his teeth when he was talking.

It wasn't at all long before he remembered the dreams of Ann and saw how extremely selective they were; to the effect that she was present in the dreams and absent in reality. An insistent phrase pressed itself upon him: I couldn't have been more of a pig. He knew very well that an attempt to make something perfect—a love that would not exclude towers and romantic riskings of the neck—had turned swiftly into a regular fuck-up flambeau, staggering even in memory. No, he thought, it must be that I couldn't have been more of a pig.

Soon enough, he went on a cheerless regime of mineral oil and a soft low-residue diet. Nevertheless, early in the second day, after half a dozen Sitz baths had restored the firmer edges to his personality, he found it necessary to adjourn to the bathroom for his first postoperative bowel movement.

Why go into such a nightmare? A single enormous turd explored every surgical error Proctor had made. Somewhat to his own discredit, Payne howled like the Anti-Christ.

And when he heard Proctor and the nurse muddling around the room outside the john, he booted the door open exactly as he had booted open the door on his grandfather's disused farmstead, shamelessly revealing himself in an exhibit of fearful squattery and tragically droned, *"You bastards core me like an apple and let me have a hard stool two days later! That makes me laugh my God that makes me laugh!"*

He wouldn't shut up though he could see Ann snapping away with her Nikon. Next to his bed, wet roses soaked on a newspaper; the note was hers: *"This is it."*

Ann looking in at this ashen, pooping, howling form felt, thus early in her career, a grave seepage of idealism, an invidious pissing away of all that was good and held meaning. She found herself staring out the window past the parking lot and the blackened contours of asphalt, past the lunatic geometry of Key West roofs to the dynamo sky of America; and turned to smile inwardly; hers was one dream that wouldn't get off the ground.

It was a pleasure to sit at the wheel, the diesels not straining, and listen to the ship-to-shore. The captain found on a clear night like tonight he could pick up the other boats as far off as the Cay Sal Bank. After a month in the Tortugas and Marquesas and a week or two violating the nursery ground, he was ready to go back to Galveston. Where he was known.

"You don't figure she'd use the camera to blackmail no one?"

The mate who looked more and more like a hillbilly song star the more the running lights accentuated his face's declivities, said, "Of course not, Captain. This here is just some sort of adventurer." The captain got up happy.

"Steady as she goes," he said to the mate, who took the wheel with a gravity that was possibly not genuine. He waited for the captain to head for the lighted companionway. "If you want yer trousers pressed, skipper, why the winch would be an awful good spot to leave them," he said, bringing down the house.

It was a starry night going to Galveston with the boom of the big trawler swaying a black metronomic line over the silver fan of wake.

And it was real life out there on the Gulf of Mexico; because down in the hold of a Key West shrimper, a person of culture was committing experience.

The tower went up with embarrassing speed and now it was Saturday on Mente Chica Key. The bats had all been dyed day-glo orange so that their bug scavenging circulation would be plain to all. Confined by a single polyethelene sheet, every last one of them was sealed in the tower.

There was a blue satin ribbon tied about the base of the tower. The tower itself stood stern and mighty and impervious to termites against the Seminole sky. Around its base, the Mid-Keys Boosters stirred by the hundreds in anticipation. There were many military personnel in Polynesian mufti. There were many retired persons of legendary mediocrity known locally as "just people." There were many snapping camera pests from the newspapers.

All around the area, the mangroves released their primitive smell and made expanses of standing water where billions upon billions of the little dark awful salt-water mosquitoes would be born *in perpetuum*, bats or no bats, quite honestly.

Nicholas Payne and C. J. Clovis flanked Dexter Fibb, aging Grand Master of the Mid-Keys Boosters, and explained how he must yank the manila rope, how he must bring down the polyethylene sheet to release the bats so that they might begin devouring the mosquitoes that this minute were making every spectator's head lumpy. Payne, unable to accustom himself to a sanitary napkin, shifted about irritably.

Dexter Fibb crushed his worn blue-and-gold yachtsman's hat about his ears, preparing himself for action, should it come his way.

As anyone could have seen by looking into their eyes, Clovis and Payne were flush with the seventeen thousand.

The dedication of the bat tower was seen as a great chance to cement the U. S. Navy's relationships with the Downtown Merchants' Association. So there were any number of Mister Fix-It types of formidable rank, often chief petty officer, on loan from the base. These helpers, enclouded by mosquitoes, gathered around bits of electronic gear, loudspeakers, strobes and emergency gadgets, sonic shark repellants and smoke bombs for attracting helicopters. One group, ordinarily employed maintaining the kind of fighter planes Doctor Proctor himself had flown, had erected a banner over their project that read:

PHANTOM PHIXERS

Some of the wives had laid out tables of country fixings, jams and jellies and whatnot, in a sentimental materialization of the kind of quasi-rural bonhomie that seemed a millimeter from actual goose-stepping and brown-shirt uproars of bumpkin fascism.

Payne moved through, scared to death. He saw the tower and the old wagon beneath, the bats whirring, vortical. The mosquitoes were definitely a problem. One reason the bats were whirring, vortical, and not sleeping was that the mosquitoes were biting them all the time and the bats couldn't do a thing about it.

To show that their husbands had gotten priority tours, some of the Navy wives wore grass skirts and red bandana tops. Beyond their muscular shoulders you could see the tower, the crowd, the whirring bat wagon, the mangroves and the hot glistening sky. Kids pegged rocks at the bat wagon and everyone swatted and dervished in clouds of mosquitoes.

One of the husbands, a chief petty officer, darkened his crew cut with an oily hand and said to mid-air: "This oscillator is givin me a fit." The chief's wife was reading the newspaper.

"Listen ta this what Pola Negri has to say: 'I was the star who introduced sex to the screen but I don't like nudity and obscenity in today's films. Movies *and* men were more romantic in my day.' I buy that."

"I do too, honey," said the chief, "but I haven't got time to think about it. Do you read me? I've got this oscillator and that rectifier back at the hangar I was mentioning which is causing me to throw a fit."

Payne was all ears. The wife saw and addressed her remarks to him.

"Don is trying to make E9 before he retires," the wife informed Payne, "then he is going to open a TV repair on Big Coppitt Key."

"What I don't have time to think about," said Don, the chief petty officer, "that is, if I am ever gonna operate a TV repair on Big Coppitt, is Pola Negri's sex life."

"Although Don would agree, wouldn't you Hon, that things in movies has got way out of line."

"I haven't got time for a bunch of beaver shows," Don told simply everybody, "Pola Negri's or anybody else's. I got this oscillator on the blink, frankly."

"What's it for?" Payne asked politely.

"Well, it's not for nothing if it's on the blink," said Don. "You follow that, don't you?"

206

"Yes . . ."

"And the rest I can't explain unless you got a U.S. of America Navy rate in electronics which you don't."

Payne wandered away without reply. He felt, somehow, that he was in no position to start skirmishes around here. But that wasn't enough; the chief followed him. "Me'n the wife," he said brazenly, "think you're takin this outfit to the cleaners."

"The cleaners?"

"That's right. I have had a look at the tab. There's quite the margin of profit."

"How much would you say?"

"Two-thirds."

"Way off."

"Am I?"

"I'm afraid you have no head for economics. *Econ* as we used to say."

"Uh huh. You know, us ordinree citizens has about had it with being milked all the time."

"You're not being milked."

"We're being milked. Don't contradict me."

"You're being taken to the cleaners," Payne corrected. "And if you had something going on in your head besides a few gummy notions of how to work less and keep the old lady in Monkey Ward's pedal-pushers and plastic bath clogs, you'd *never* get taken. Now, unless you want to come out and play with the grown-ups, I suggest you quit whining and go back to fixing wires for the U.S. of America Navy before you spoil your credit with them. Isn't all that many outfits have room for you time-servers."

The chief came very close, squinting. He waved a whole handful of fingers slowly in Payne's face. He tilted his head. "Amo tell you one thing sumbitch; if I see a way to come in on you, amo take it." The not quite pitiable swab was worked up to the point that, with any more goading, he would have had a philosophical outburst with references to the nation and its perpetrating enemies. There seemed to be no cure for pests like Payne but automotive decals and secret handshakes. The freaks were coming out of the woodwork.

Payne joined Clovis at the tower where the two of them greeted the faithful. Payne stood beside him with an easy winning grin and waited for the group to clear. "Do you get the feeling they're on to us?" he asked with a smile for a small lady gorged with potato salad who yoo-hooed from the mangroves, flapping at a cloud of insects with a red plastic picnic fork.

"Sure do," Clovis smiled to them all. "Let's just hope we can keep it glued together until the ceremony is over. I notice you're limping."

Some moments later, the chief petty officer of various electrical pursuits came toward the tower, only to set up the loudspeakers that would amplify Clovis' singular voice. Nevertheless, he made Payne nervous. Payne had begun to regret his speech about taking people to the cleaners; and, in fact, had lost what little interest he had had in the money; so that he was in a very bleak frame of mind about their prospects.

He had too a tremor of agony that some child would come up and tell him he hoped these bats would do the job because his baby sister was dying of encephalitis. Here, son, here's all the grimy loot we chiseled out of your dad and his neighbors and here are the keys to my Hudson Hornet and that Dodge Motor Home over there. Wire me collect, Leavenworth, if you have motor trouble. I'm cashing in. My soul is all shot to shit and I don't know where I get off next. *I am penitent,* Payne thought, *I have brought this upon myself.*

Dexter Fibb, at fifty-three, had never had a moving violation. He had never declined a luncheon speech at the Lions and he had never hesitated to dry the dishes or take out the garbage when he was asked to do so by his wife, Bambi.

Dexter Fibb loved symmetry. He loved the bat tower because it was symmetrical and he loved Bambi because her whopping bust was the same size as her gibbous backside. Dexter Fibb often grew upset with himself when he tried to cut his sideburns to the same length, and would advance them millimeter by millimeter until they were small indentations above his ears. He could never get his sleeves right when he rolled them up either; one would always be somewhat farther down on his elbow than the other and on those unfortunate mornings that he would button his shirt out of line, he would rip it from his body with a shriek and fish another heavily starched white-on-white see-thru from his top drawer.

Fibb believed in many things that verged upon superstition but which helped him through a world in which he seemed to lack some essential spiritual coordination. He read *Consumer's Digest* and evaluated his friends' cars by looking at the color of the exhaust pipe. His favorite automobile was that old model Studebaker that seemed to go backward and forward all at once.

The pilot committee of the Mid-Keys Boosters bought the bat tower mainly because Fibb made so much of its looking the same from any angle. And it is to his love of symmetry that we must ascribe his instantaneous horror at the sight of C. J. Clovis.

On the sound truck next to the door, leaking wires into the hands of the electric petty officer, this sign:

OUR GOD IS NOT DEAD.
SORRY ABOUT YOURS.

"How's she goin, Don?" Fibb asked the CPO.

"Real good, Dexter. I had this oscillator givin me a fit but I isolated the sumbitch with a circuit tester."

Fibb went inconspicuously to the microphone, still disconnected and, half-preoccupied, tried to warm it up. He did a couple of licks from old Arthur Godfrey and Paul Harvey shows. He did a quick Lipton Noodle Soup take and smiled to remember the old applause-meter. A couple of the muscular hula ladies wandered by and Fibb got randy.

He sat on the platform, waving mosquitoes away with the want-ads from the *Key West Citizen*, and tried to think what he would say. Another hula lady went by and Fibb thought how he would like to slip it to her, right in the old flange, where it counted, by God.

The chief pulled a plastic ukulele out of his truck and strummed at her wildly without effect. "You're a damn lightnin fingers," Fibb told him.

"I own every record Les Paul and Mary Ford ever cut. My wife's got all the Hugo Winterhalters. And have I got the Hi-fi. Crackerjack little sumbitch I grabbed cheap on my last tour. Diamond needle, sumbitchin speakers waist-high, AM, FM, the whole shootin match."

Dexter Fibb spotted C. J. Clovis looking just especially grotesque, all by himself, with that aluminum understructure sticking out of everywhere. He winced.

"Kind of pathetic, ain't he?" inquired the chief.

"Some people just don't draw lucky," said Dexter Fibb with some strain, watching Clovis hitch across the field.

"I don't know, Dexter. I think he come up with a handful on this go-round."

"Oh, God, who's to say, who's to say," said Fibb, eyes askew.

The chief said with craft, "Would you just want me to estimate the rake-off for you? I have a little background in econ, Dex. I could show you . . ."

The generosity of the Navy was considerable. A parking problem which had begun to look acute was quickly alleviated by the arrival of four MPs whose training showed immediately. The incoming mass of automobiles magically became rows of parked cars with walking lanes in-between that permitted people to move directly to the stage and tower.

Clovis met Payne at the bat wagon. Payne talked to a booster who was handing out ice-cream parlor fans. He limped over to Clovis, gesturing to him with his head.

"They want you to speak," said Clovis. "I told them you were a lawyer."

"Why?"

"Because I didn't want any loose legal questioning. I wanted them to figure you as an expert."

"Oh, God, I don't think I can make a speech."

"You plain have to. You make one before they open the tower and I'll do the wind-up. Hell, that'll give you a chance to get to your car before I do."

"No," said Payne the sport, "I'd wait for you." He couldn't think of a thing he could tell these people, except possibly that they'd been had.

But when the time came for him to speak, he climbed up on the platform not only ready but with a sense of mission. At his very appearance, a shimmer of antagonism passed through the crowd; and when, in his introductory remarks, he referred to beer as "the nectar of the gobs," he was actually booed, if only a little. He began to wonder exactly how he would handle himself if the crowd decided to work him over. "Beer then," he said after his joke was badly received. "Have some beer." Silence. You bastards, he thought: very well. I will win them over.

"Let me be quite frank with you," he lied. "I'd like to say that even though I don't recognize a face out here except that of my partner, I feel as if I've known you all. Everything here has reminded me of you folks. Not so much the tower as the potato salad you folks been eatin out chere." He thought he'd try a little Delta gumbo-mouth on them. "Do you know what I mean? Last night I listened to a nigra militant on TV, talking about what he called blapp people and gee as I look around I see this community is entirely short of blapp people. Not only blapp people but weirdos." The sympathetic chuckle that ensued put him entirely out of reach of hecklers. "Why God, you're the secret honky underground network of America!" Applause. "And I don't see any backs up against any walls!" More applause. "Why it's solid potato salad out there!" The applause this time was uncertain.

"Well, now. Next time you're recollecting this day, *as you will*, just remember that you bought yourselves a bat tower and all the freaks and weirdos and agitators and blapp people didn't!" Wild, bewildered applause.

"I'm just awful afraid the aforementioned citizens didn't buy a bat tower at all!"

"*NO!*" from the crowd.

"But you doozies with your prickly heads and hush-puppy shoes sure bought one!"

"*Hurray!*"

"I was just telling this chief petty officer a few minutes ago. You people have been taken to the cleaners!" A good-natured, superior murmur passed over the potato salad. *"You've been fleeced!"*

"HURRAY! HURRAY! HURRAY!"

Clovis, ashen, passed Payne on his way to the microphone. "You've got moxie," he offered, "I'll say that." Then he added: "In another hour, A1A will be a fugitive's bottleneck." Payne limped off, patting his pocket. The wad of money was as big as a pistol.

Dexter Fibb received Clovis on the podium, unable to touch him or shake his hand or really take in with his eyes Clovis' implausible lack of symmetry. Moreover, Fibb was miffed that he had not himself been asked to speak.

The crowd, too, was sobered by the sight of the multiple amputee. "My partner's slighting remarks," he began, "about *minority groups* are not necessarily the opinion of the management. Ahaha. Ahmm." As far as the crowd was concerned, Clovis was a dead man. "You're ah you're a um a really great audience folks!" Then simply, humbly, "And a much appreciated customer." He smiled, head bowed, awaiting the kind of response Payne had gotten. It never came. Better speed things up. Better speed them right the fuck up before this dude comes down like a bomb.

The potato salad had begun to stir. Dexter Fibb nervously crushed his worn blue-and-gold yachtsman's cap about his ears, preparing himself for action, and cried, "Let's put these bats to work!"

Clovis suddenly and almost spasmodically went into his speech about encephalitis and about how bats were like little angels and how mosquitoes were like flying pus-filled syringes. But he ran down like a child's gyroscope. His face, at last, revealed his defeat.

Only Payne was able to start the applause—a strange

noise like breaking waves. The vacant faces were intent with the motion of their hands beneath them. It surged through the mangroves in a gesture of confidence and of more than that: of faith.

Ultimately, though, looking into all those hopeful vacant faces gathered at this tower from every corner of the U.S.A., his own flush with the purloined funds and a special joy that went beyond that, Clovis snipped as he must with heavy shears the blue satin ribbon. Dexter Fibb gave a self-conscious rebel yell, got a red face and pulled the rope. The polyethylene came down the sides of the tower, caressing it as it went, lofting and flowing in wind-borne plastic beauty. Bright orange bats poured into the sky.

They were scattered at first, just as they ought to have been, circulating in the immediate area. But then they began to form up. A single shape, more demonstrative than an arrow, in a color derived from every neon monstrosity in the land, formed on the soaring sky at the edge of America. All the hopes of all those empty faces were pinned to that shape that held brilliant overhead a moment more then headed for the interior of the continent and disappeared.

Quite rightly, the wail went up: *"They're gone! They're gone forever! They won't ever come back!"* and so on.

And when the anguish had passed, the potato salad began to advance upon the podium. Dexter Fibb, seeing slippery-looking Payne and the horrifically malformed Clovis, cued the crowd with outraged glances at the two. A serious question with its roots deep in Econ had arisen.

With the first movement of the crowd toward him, Clovis fell to the boards, dragging the Telefunken microphone after himself, convenient to his lips. The great port-

214

able speakers transmitted his gasps and howls: *"MY HEART IS ON THE FRITZ!"* It was amplified over the sea of bat fans, bug loathers and mangroves. *"THE FRITZ I SAID!"*

Croaking even more impressively than Clovis, Dexter Fibb cried, "Look at him, he's dying!" and stared pale and mute at this crooked item on the stage. Payne listened to Clovis perform extravagantly at the microphone, bleating a ravaged play-by-play as to the condition of his ticker. Payne knelt consolingly beside him. Clovis glanced at him, simulated a grisly death rattle, looked at Payne once again in surprise, looked all around himself and said, "No." Then, without further notice, he died quite blankly.

Payne was the solitary customer at the burial. Though, because of some logistical miscalculation, row upon row of empty folding chairs faced the oblong black hole in the sod. Overhead, a green and white canopy—a pavilion— was turn-buckled tautly on a galvanized pipe frame. Four men took the coffin, a piece of mildly pretentious metal furniture containing the jury-rigged mortal remains of C. J. Clovis, and lowered away. Payne sat on a folding chair, his legs crossed tight on themselves, leaned his face heavily into his hands and thought, "Oh, gee. Oh, fuck."

Payne stayed, after the four men left, in the big open cemetery. The skeletal Poinciana trees stood upon an enormous ocean sky with tenuous, high-altitude horsetail clouds. Key West, a clapboard town accreted upon a marine hummock at the end of the continental shelf, seemed a peculiar place to have buried Clovis, who had entrusted himself to Payne. Overhead, a pair of frigate birds circled in perfect synchronization as though fixed to the ends of a glass fulcrum.

Payne was tapped gently upon the shoulder by a recent graduate of the police academy who said, "You are under arrest."

"What is the charge?"

"Fraud."

In the police cruiser, Payne quietly began to slip a little. They drove past the cryptic gestures of docks, careened trawlers and crawfishing boats of Garrison Bight. They passed the breaking Atlantic at the foot of Simonton Street. "Take me to the Burger King," he told the cop without getting an answer. "Officer, what you see before you is a futuristic print-out of a thousand years of bog-trotting and one boat ride to an experimental republic: a fiasco." *Silence*. It was dizzying to Payne. From the inside of a police sedan, Payne believed he could see a vast and unplowed interior ridge, buried beneath flags, gum wrappers and diplomas. "I have found my swerve, officer. It makes a gentle glowing contour on the history of the New World." This hero, Nicholas Payne, began smiling. He had the oceanic feeling a thousand yards from sea. The lowering of one defunct sensorium into the sod still filled his head with the martial music of winds and supermarkets, a fugue of singing trees and internal combustion engines, of Miss America contestants past and present doing night things with sturdy flutes, an international autoharmonium of homocidal giddiness manipulated by played-out bobby soxers and sharp dressers in security councils and command modules; it was all out there, the unplowed ridge where energetic riders on winded ponies were impeded by hairdressers with bullwhips, tigerish insurance adjusters, rodents in command formation and other servants of the commonwealth. The last thing Payne said to the perplexed young policeman was, *"To me he was illustrious."*

. .

By returning most of the money, the small discrepancy justified by the touristic utility of the empty tower, Payne avoided the brunt of sentencing. And finally, it was agreed that if he would re-enact his trial for the TV program *Night Court*, he would be let free altogether.

Payne walked into the studio. Two or three technicians wandered around trailing rubber cables and, finally, rolling a camera forward on its dolly to face a plywood judge's bench. The "Judge" himself came in a few moments later and prated in a resonating actor's voice that if Equity found out what he was getting for this bit they'd have him in the slammer so fast his head would swim. Once seated, his judicial mien returned and he was given a "policeman" who declared court was in session. Payne felt as if he were in a dream. He watched a man tried for manslaughter do some wonderful Karl Malden stuff, his upper lip whitening with the tension of vigorous speeches, slobbering with Actor's Studio reality an ad-lib monologue that had the technicians winking at each other.

Then Payne, dreaming, was called, and subsequently so were the witnesses against him. The charge was fraud. The witnesses were Dexter Fibb and five Mid-Keys Boosters, including the chief petty officer, all on TV for the first time.

When they got to the death of Clovis, Payne burst into his only tears since the actuality, a weeping sleepwalker. He looked around himself, saw the trial as though through glass. The judge tried not to beam. The director crowded behind the cameramen to see this. *Night Court,* rich with corrective lessons, was a hit.

Let's have this quickly now: At Galveston, Ann wired for money, a lot of it, waited three hours, got it, flew to

217

Dallas, took a room, called George and gave him the *yes* he had waited for so many years. Hearing his tears, his gratitude, she made reservations on Delta to fly up the next day; then, headed for Neiman-Marcus.

So that: She ran across the tarmac at Detroit-Metropolitan Airport, adorable in a little mini-caftan by Oscar de la Renta made of pink linen. Over that she wore a delicate Moroccan leather coat. The sandals were Dior; and their blocky little heels looked like ivory. Anyone who says she wasn't darling has another think coming.

And George ran to her perfectly attired in an impeccably tailored glen plaid from J. Press. What seemed almost risky in his livery was the wild, yellow Pucci cravat that precisely counterpointed his sedate, seamless cordovans from Church of London.

See them, then, running thus toward one another: perfect monads of nullity.

They whirled in one another's arms.

"Darling," Ann said, "I've been through much." She had caught a little cold aboard ship and George was very, very concerned. After gathering her luggage, they went directly to a hotel where George greedily massaged her chest with Vick's Vap-O-Rub.

It is quite true that George hired the gallery. Nevertheless, Ann's first show was reviewed legitimately; and was a success. Probably the quarterly critic, Allan Lier, of *Lens* magazine, represents the consensus:

. . . Miss Fitzgerald's striking available-light photographs of commercial fishermen turning in for the night are the best sequence of the show. Frame after frame, we see these tired men backlit against the hatchway, heading for a long-earned rest. In their impatience and exhaustion, they are already in various stages of undress.

By way of contrast, the group of pictures called "Nicholas" introduces us to a private yet utterly communicated vision of what is lost in the conventional life. We see time and time again the same weary face of Nicholas: the 'shy suitor,' the spurious rodeo cowboy, the motorist. In one superb shot, in a claustrophobic laundry room, Nicholas is drubbed over the head with a toilet plunger by an attractive older woman: It is left to the viewer to speculate as to what he has done to deserve this! In another picture, he stares directly into the camera, apparently about to speak but unable to think of a single thing to say. In the most terrifying picture of them all, he rises from a toilet seeming to spring at the camera. He wears a short institutional shift and we see where his mediocrity leads. Nothing that is said here can communicate the banality which Miss Fitzgerald captures with polish and control. Thanks to her craft, humanity and attention, she has delivered a cautionary monument to the failed life.

See this show at once.

Payne headed North, making two stops in the State of Florida. One was to see Junior Place and inspect the bat cave with him; the tower bats had not been rejected by their friends and hung upside down from the roof of the cave like thousands of Indian River oranges.

He stopped on the Georgia border and bought an M. Hohner Marine Band harmonica and spent the better part of an evening failing to play Hank Williams' "I'll Never Get Out Of This World Alive."

A truck drove by with a sign: HOLD UP YOUR PACK OF AMERICAN SPACE. The question was whether he had actually seen that. That was getting to be the real question all right.

On a lonely beach in the Sea Islands, Nicholas Payne unfolded his camp stove and began to prepare his supper. He could smell the sea and the sandy groves of loblolly pine that throbbed with uncommon birds. Turned at an angle to the homemade trailer whose floor smelled balefully of departed bats, the Hudson Hornet pointed to the interior of the continent.

Payne poised a jacknife spread with peanut butter over a rigid piece of bread and lifted his face to the sea. He felt as if he had been made an example of; and that, even now, he was part of a demonstration, an exhibit. He held the knife and peanut butter steady. The sky rose over him, round and vitreous, a glass enclosure. He smiled, at one with things. He knew the great blenders hummed in state centers and benign institutions; while he, far away, put it all together at a time when life was cheap.

But then the abrasions, all the incredible abrasions, had *rendered* him. The pale, final shape of Payne, like the yolk of an egg held to the light, had come to be seen.

I am at large.

Also available from Minerva

Neil Bissoondath

A CASUAL BRUTALITY

"In Neil Bissoondath's fine new novel, the atmosphere of paranoia and tension created by the death-throes of a short-lived financial boom on the small Caribbean island of Casaquemada is sustained throughout by a tone which is both passionate and ironic . . .

"As the story of a Casaquemadan doctor, Ramsingh, returning from Canada, progresses, his gradual induction into the reality of living in an increasingly anarchic and unstable society is conveyed in sharp jolts of incident.

"*A Casual Brutality* is very much a description of colonialism gone wrong . . . The false economic boom on Casaquemada has become like a cancer: the island is dying but a 'cure' would almost certainly kill. It is this dilemma that Bissoondath writes about with great sensitivity and realism"   *Guardian*

"A marvellously assured performance"
Financial Times

"The book builds to a shattering climax. Like Naipaul, Bissoondath is excellent at atmosphere, at place, at detail"   Hanif Kureishi, *New Statesman*

"An absorbing and very readable novel written with intelligence, conviction and wit . . . 'Promise', the usual word for first novels, would be an insult here; this important book is a complete, mature achievement"   Hilary Mantel, *Weekend Telegraph*

"A disturbing, original voice"   *Independent*

Robert Coover

WHATEVER HAPPENED TO GLOOMY GUS OF THE CHICAGO BEARS?

This is the account of the last great run on Memorial Day, 1937, by that legendary all-American of the grid-iron and the bed, Gloomy Gus, alias Iron Butt, also known as Dick to friends and family back in Whittier, California. It is the story of the American Dream, as acted out by the Fighting Quaker ("I believe in the American dream," he has said, "because I have seen it come true in my own life!") and as narrated by an orphaned Russian Jew named Meyer, a part-time union organizer and WPA sculptor with a studio in an old warehouse said to have been used as a liquor depot by Bugs Moran's gang in Chicago's Old Town District.

This bawdy, iconoclastic yet celebrative work is reminiscent of Robert Coover's *A Political Fable (The Cat In The Hat For President)* and his epic masterpiece *The Public Burning*, and adds a new and hilarious twist to the myth of America.

"An astonishing work . . . along with Vonnegut's *Bluebeard*, this is the finest new work of fiction you are likely to find this year" *City Limits*

"An elegant, amusing and complex satire on macho myths and the politics of fame and perfect technique" *Spectator*

"A hugely entertaining novel" *TLS*

A Selected List of Titles Available in Minerva

While every effort is made to keep prices low, it is sometimes necessary to increase prices at short notice. Mandarin Paperbacks reserves the right to show new retail prices on covers which may differ from those previously advertised in the text or elsewhere.

The prices shown below were correct at the time of going to press.

Fiction

☐	7493 9009 3	**The Holy Innocents**	Gilbert Adair	£3.99 BX
☐	7493 9006 9	**The Tidewater Tales**	John Barth	£4.99 BX
☐	7493 9004 2	**A Casual Brutality**	Neil Bissoondath	£4.50 BX
☐	7493 9018 2	**Interior**	Justin Cartwright	£3.99 BC
☐	7493 9002 6	**No Telephone to Heaven**	Michelle Cliff	£3.99 BX
☐	7493 9000 X	**Faces and Masks**	Eduardo Galeano	£4.99 BX
☐	7493 9011 5	**Parable of the Blind**	Gert Hofmann	£3.99 BC
☐	7493 9010 7	**The Inventor**	Jakov Lind	£3.99 BC
☐	7493 9003 4	**Fall of the Imam**	Nawal El Saadawi	£3.99 BC

Non-Fiction

☐	7493 9012 3	**Days in the Life**	Jonathon Green	£4.99 BC
☐	7493 9019 0	**In Search of J D Salinger**	Ian Hamilton	£4.50 BX
☐	7493 9023 9	**Stealing from a Deep Place**	Brian Hall	£3.99 BX
☐	7493 9005 0	**The Orton Diaries**	John Lahr	£4.99 BC
☐	7493 9014 X	**Nora**	Brenda Maddox	£5.99 BC

All these books are available at your bookshop or newsagent, or can be ordered direct from the publisher. Just tick the titles you want and fill in the form below. Available in:
BX: British Commonwealth excluding Canada
BC: British Commonwealth including Canada

Mandarin Paperbacks, Cash Sales Department, PO Box 11, Falmouth, Cornwall TR10 9EN.

Please send cheque or postal order, no currency, for purchase price quoted and allow the following for postage and packing:

UK	55p for the first book, 22p for the second book and 14p for each additional book ordered to a maximum charge of £1.75.
BFPO and Eire	55p for the first book, 22p for the second book and 14p for each of the next seven books, thereafter 8p per book.
Overseas Customers	£1.00 for the first book plus 25p per copy for each additional book.

NAME (Block Letters) ....

ADDRESS ....

....